HUGH: BLUE BLOOD COMPELLED

THE BLUE BLOOD RETURNS SERIES, BOOK 2

STACY EATON

CHAPTER ONE

HUGH

1 Year Earlier

I took a seat at my desk, glancing over my small work area to see if anything new was there. Not that I expected anything; it was rare to have any type of paper left on our desks. Most of our stuff landed on our phones or virtual tablets. Even my voicemails from the office line went to my cell-phone. However, we did have quite a few storerooms full of metal cabinets that had folders in them and a shit ton of boxes with printed copies of reports, photographs, and other evidence that had accumulated over the years.

Evidence was now collected and scanned into images and stored on one of our secure servers. Once that was done, it was triple-checked to make sure that all the identifying marks were collected properly before destroying the physical evidence. If a piece of evidence were needed for prosecution, it would be rendered again with machines to make it look identical to the original, then recycled. There was no wasted space for weapons and drugs. All interviews were also done through video and sometimes audio methods.

I couldn't imagine how law enforcement in the past had kept everything straight when it was all on paper. Even things typed into the computers were printed out and stuffed into binders or folders. It boggled my mind how much had changed in the last twenty-five years.

The concept of digging through those folders full of information to find a specific detail was utterly foreign to me. These days, we could search for a keyword, and the computer would bring up anything that would be valid to our case. As we investigated, we added the audio and video along with any crime scene details, persons involved, and photographs. Then the computer system would tell us what we needed to do next. It also helped connect dots that we might not have seen otherwise. Plus, we were always in touch with our cases and our bosses— well, sometimes a little too much on that last part.

I heard someone approaching and looked up to see Bruce Cochran, my sometimes partner, heading toward his desk. "Morning, Murph. You're here early."

"Yeah, not sleeping so well these days."

He smirked. "Jocelyn keeping you up?"

"Nah, we split up a few months ago. I think it's because I'm getting old. I don't seem to need as much sleep as I used to."

"Murph, you're not even forty yet; you're not old." He grinned at me. "Wait till you're my age, and then we can talk. Besides, not sleeping has nothing to do with age. I'm forty-five, and I sleep like a baby."

"I hear you."

"Hey," he said as he took a seat at his desk. "Did you see the news this morning? Two more massacres overnight."

"Wait, two? I heard about the one in New York City, but where was the other one? Or were they connected?"

"No, there was another one in Atlanta. The news was talking about how they are comparing these to the active shooter rampages they used to have in the early two-thousands."

"Well, shit, that's not good."

"I know." He shook his head. "They need to figure out a way to keep those fucking creepy creatures in check. We should round them all up and slaughter every last one of them."

I frowned. "Why do you say that?"

"Because they are blood-sucking freaks, that's why!" He laughed as he took a seat.

"Yes, but they have been around a lot longer than we have. Maybe we are the freaks. You don't see any of them overweight and with a ton of medical problems."

He stared at me and then flopped back in his seat. "Holy shit, you're a vamp-fan."

I put my hand up. "Hold on a second; I'm not saying I'm a fan. I'm saying that they have been around for a very long time, and we are just coming to learn about them. How have they stayed hidden for so long? Think about that. Until recently, they kept to themselves. Yeah, we'd seen and heard about some weird shit that happened that we couldn't quite explain, but they weren't in-your-face about their business."

"True, but now they are."

"Don't you wonder what has changed?" I had thought about that quite a bit recently. Truth be told, it had been on my mind more often than I cared to admit. As far as I knew, vampires had been around since the dawn of time. The fact that their existence was now public knowledge was slightly awe-inspiring.

Yes, they were deadly creatures, as we had all come to learn very quickly, but they intrigued me. What had their lives been like all these years? How had they stayed under our radar? Why stay under the radar? What was happening in their world for them to come forward and make themselves known now?

Bruce broke me out of my reverie. "Who cares what changed. What I want to know is how we are going to get rid of them."

"Seriously? Aren't you the least bit interested in learning more about them?"

"Fuck, no!"

"See, I am. I find the fact that these people have been living amongst us for all these years rather fascinating. How could we not have known? Maybe some people did, but the majority of people didn't. It makes me wonder what else is out there."

He stared at me funny. "What? You mean like werewolves and elves and demons and shit?"

"Who knows." I shrugged. "If vampires exist, maybe they do too."

He sneered. "Let's hope the hell not. One nasty creature is enough to deal with, and I can't believe you referred to them as people. They are far from civilized human beings."

I was about to comment on that when all the virtual screens in the office flashed and then beeped, alerting us to an incoming message. "All agents are requested to attend the meeting at nine a.m. sharp. Please acknowledge your receipt of this message." Our boss' voice came from the speakers, and Bruce and I looked at one another.

"Wow, been a long time since we were all called into a meeting," Bruce said. "I wonder what's up."

"It probably has to do with what happened last night," I replied. "Maybe they want us to prepare for that to happen here in Philly."

"Maybe." He pushed a button on his virtual screen to acknowledge the message, and I did the same before I glanced at my watch to see it was still before eight. I had enough time to go over my to-do list and see what needed my attention before the meeting.

Five minutes before nine, another announcement rang through the room, reminding everyone about the meeting, and several of the agents began to converge on the stairs to head down a floor to our conference room. Bruce and I joined the group, and I listened to the mutterings of those around me as they all tried to guess what the topic of the meeting would be.

We had known about the vampire race for less than two years, and when we had first learned about them, everyone was up in arms. The news media went wild with footage of their killing sprees, and the general human population had been running scared. Many were locking themselves into their homes with fear of going out in public. It sounded similar to how the people had reacted back when the COVID-19 virus went viral, and the pandemic shocked the world. I was just an infant then, but I'd learned about it in school. A massive quarantine order had been put into effect, and for months people stayed inside while fear ran rampant through the world.

It was like that after their presence became known. Some humans had come forward to say they had been aware of the vampires' existence for a while, and they defended them as a peaceful society that had been existing amongst us for hundreds, if not thousands, of years. While the stories had been never-ending, few facts had been shared with us and even less that were confirmed.

The conference room filled with over a hundred agents, and Bruce and I glanced at one another questioningly. I had expected our floor to be here but didn't expect the entire building of agents to be present.

Our boss, Steve Windwood, stood at the front of the room with Zack Easlick, the head of Immigration. What the hell were these two doing together? While we did work with ICE occasionally on homeland terror cells, we didn't generally meet up with one another at this level.

"Alright, can I have everybody's attention," Steve spoke into the microphone in front of him. "I know you all have a lot to do, so let's get this over with quickly."

The room grew quiet as everyone gave him their attention.

"You all know Zack Easlick from ICE. We have been

working together on a new project, and it's time to make that project common knowledge and build a solid task force. Over the last couple of months, we have seen the rise in violence with this new species—you know, the vampires. The violence is expanding and not just in our major cities but in our small towns. It doesn't stop there either; it is the same around the globe. We have all witnessed the carnage either personally or via video footage, but it is time that we get a handle on this situation. That's why we are starting a new task force that will focus solely on vampires, and those humans that work with them. This task force will not only be about dealing with the violence but what we can learn to help us understand these people—or whatever they are—and figure out what we can do to stop this and keep them in line."

Zack approached the microphone, and Steve shifted to the side. "I know you all are wondering what the hell ICE is doing here, and I sure wish we weren't, but we have learned that many of these beings are moving between countries. We also know that they have a governing body that exists in multiple countries around the world—think a United Nations kind of thing. We want to work with DHS to find out what they are up to, how they control their own, and try to stop them from any world domination plans that they might have."

I frowned as I thought about his world domination wording. I didn't believe that was their purpose, and I peered to the side to see Bruce shaking his head and leaning toward another guy on his left as he whispered something to him.

"We are looking for volunteers who want to work on this task force. Between our two agencies, we should have enough people interested in learning more and seeing what we can do to stop the violence. We have seen the damage that this race can do, and we need to figure out how to stop it or control it before it is too late."

Steve stepped forward again. "If there is anyone who wants

to be part of this task force, raise your hand. If you are even slightly interested, raise your hand so we can talk more."

My hand went up, and Bruce started laughing as he slapped my shoulder. "Figures you would, Murph."

There were about twenty-five of us that raised our hands. "Okay, those of you who have no interest, you are excused. The rest of you stay put, and we'll give you some further details."

Bruce clapped me on the shoulder again. "You have fun with that, buddy. It looks like I'll be dealing with our case alone today."

As they left, there was muttering and laughter, and those of us who stayed shifted toward the front of the room. I knew most of the people in the group, but not all. Some of them were from the forensics division, others from the technology department.

"Thank you to all of you for staying," Steve said as he stepped away from the microphone now that the group was smaller. "What we are looking for is a group of people who can work side by side with ICE agents to pull this task force together. It won't just be centered here in Philadelphia either; we will be nationwide, and we will work with other countries to share information."

"What is it that you hope to gain with this task force?" a woman from our IT department asked.

"Well, we want to know what these people are, who these people are, and what they can do. We are going to need people who aren't afraid to come face-to-face with them and are curious enough to push to get answers."

"Even the tech people?" she queried.

He nodded. "Yes, we are going to need databases built that can track, technical equipment to oversee investigations, and we're going to need people who can help us oversee engineering of weapons that can be used against them."

She nodded as did a few others. "Do you plan on having us interview these people, vampires, whatever they are?"

"Yes, we do. Just like how you would cultivate any confidential informant, we are going to need to build relationships with them to see what we can learn. We know that they have long lives; we know that for some reason, they have decided to make their world visible to us; we just don't know why. We need to know if they are planning on trying to take over the world."

I laughed. "Sir, somehow, I doubt that. If they have been around all these years—centuries—whatever, why would they decide that now was the time to take over the world?"

"I agree with you, McMurphy. I don't think that they are either. I believe something else is going on, but there are others at the top of our food chain that are concerned. We have heard rumors that they are fighting amongst themselves, and that might be what has them coming forward. Maybe whatever they are dealing with, we can help put a stop to it so that no more humans get killed in the crossfire."

"Do you think that's possible?" I asked. "I mean, I have a feeling that if they are warring against themselves, they don't care who gets killed."

He sighed. "Or they could be using us as examples. Who knows. That's the point of this whole task force. We *want* to know."

I glanced at the guy beside me, Warren Bates; we had worked a couple of cases together in the past. He seemed as interested as I did in what they were saying. We listened for a few more minutes, and then Steve told us to put in an official request to join the task force. We'd no longer carry our current caseload and would instead focus one hundred percent on the vampire race. I was totally on board.

After Steve excused everyone, he waved me toward the front. "Hugh, I'm glad you stepped forward today. I was hoping you would."

"Why is that, sir?"

"Because I'd like you to start as being the head chair of the task force for our side. You'd be working with Tom Singer from ICE to oversee everything. Would that be something you'd be interested in?"

"Wow, of course, sir, but why me?"

"Since the day that their existence became public knowledge, you have had an interest in them. You haven't appeared all gung ho to wipe them out but instead, showed an interest in learning about them. To be honest, I think there is a lot for us to learn and a whole lot more of them than we think there are. I want someone who is smart, on top of things, and isn't biased one way or the other."

"Well, I can do that, sir."

"Good, put your official transfer request in, and I'll make sure it happens. On Monday, you will report to your new office on the tenth floor. We'll get started then."

After we shook hands, I went back to my desk and opened my virtual computer to bring up our inter-office site. I filled out the form, and right before I clicked the submit button, I paused.

Did I really want to get involved with this world? Was it a sick fascination that I had, or was it something more? I wasn't sure why, but for some reason, it felt like it was more, and I clicked the send button and sat back in my chair, feeling like I was about to open Pandora's box.

CHAPTER TWO

HUGH

*B*y three weeks in, we had a proper setup going. There were twenty-one of us in my group, and nineteen in Tom's. We were on the same floor in the building but opposite sides. We had several people from both groups that worked together and focused on technical aspects. There were another few people that focused on forensic possibilities for the future. The rest of us divided into groups that were focusing on different parts of the country.

Our first task was to try and determine the number of vampires that were in our country. While we did that, we were also trying to ascertain if there was any hierarchy in place for them. Did someone control them? Did they run free to do as they please? We had mention of a government of sorts, but nothing confirmed. I had to believe that there was at least one person, if not a group of people, who did oversee them. How else would they have been able to keep their existence a secret for all these years?

Since the V-Force came together—our nickname for the task force—we have been mostly stuck inside the building. We had spent our time researching what we could from past cases and the internet. Everyone was collecting names, locations, images, characteristics, and any other information that they deemed could potentially be beneficial to us.

As of now, we had over two hundred suspected vampires recorded, and I had a feeling that we had barely scratched the surface. We had divided the country into four sections to go with the time zones. It seemed the easiest way to do it right now until we could figure out where the most significant populations were situated. Once we did that, we could regroup and rezone our areas.

So far, we had found more significant numbers on the East Coast, but there were quite a few in the west near Arizona, Texas, and the New Mexico regions. We'd also heard rumors that Canada had started a similar task force because they too were seeing an uptick in violence. They had a large number of vampires in their northern sections of the country. Most likely to take advantage of the shorter days.

We had very little information about the species other than they did appear to drink blood, they lived a long time, and they didn't like sunlight. Did the sun kill them? We weren't one hundred percent sure, but since sightings of them were rare when the sun was up, we had to assume it affected them somehow. A few confirmed vampires had been seen outside during the day, so we knew that the sun didn't seem to make them combust into flames. There were many theories out there about that; if only we could get someone to confirm something.

I was leaving my mother's house after my weekly check-in and dinner when I noticed the neighbor's lights on. My mother had told me over dinner not too long ago that she wondered about them. She said that they were awake at all hours of the night, but she had rarely ever seen them during daylight hours.

She also stated, not for the first time, that they still looked as young as they did when they had moved in twenty years ago. They seemed kind enough, and I had spoken to them on occasion, but I didn't know them well. I had to agree with my mom; they fit the bill into the types of people we were researching. What were the chances that my mother's next-door neighbors were vampires?

I sat in my transport and stared at their house for a long moment. Was it worth checking out? Maybe. Would they admit what they were if they were indeed vampires? I guess I wouldn't know until I asked. With that decided, I climbed back out of my car and crossed the yard.

I paused at their front door and then inhaled long and slowly before releasing it and hitting the doorbell. It was only a moment before the door opened, and Bridgette Thames smiled brightly at me. "Hugh, it's been a while since we've seen you. How are you?"

"I'm well, Bridgette; how are you and Henry?"

"Very good. Is everything alright with your mother?" she asked, seemingly appropriately concerned as she peered out the door toward my mother's house.

"No, she's fine. Thank you for asking. Actually," I paused, wondering if I should make an excuse and leave, but I reminded myself that we had to cultivate friendships to learn. "I was wondering if I might ask you a personal question."

Her brows popped for a second, and then she chuckled slightly. "Let me ask you one first, Hugh. Is this business or pleasure in which you want to know the answer to the burning question?"

Was I freaked out that she seemed to have a good idea of what I wanted to talk about with her? Just a little. "Maybe a little bit of both, but I think tonight, it's more personal."

She grinned at me and pulled open the door. Her long dark hair cascaded over her slim shoulders, and she wore a flowy blouse and skirt and was barefoot. The perfume that she wore smelled of lilacs, and I only knew that scent because it was my mother's favorite flower. "Well, this might be a conversation that should take place inside. Why don't you come in."

I studied her face for a moment longer, and it was evident that she knew why I was here. That made me curious, and that's why I stepped over the threshold. "Bridgette, you act like you know what I want to talk to you about."

She shrugged, a sexy smile crossing her lips as she tilted her head my way. "Maybe I do. I have a feeling that you are going to ask me if my husband and I are vampires. Is that correct?"

"Why would you assume that was what I was going to ask you?"

She closed the door, shifting closer to me as she did. Her brown eyes glinted with humor as she leaned forward and spoke softly. "Because you have that look all over your face, and you are slightly nervous. I can smell your fear."

What did fear smell like? I swallowed. "So, you are?"

She laughed a delicate sound that made me look at her closer. She was stunning, and her face had flawless glowing skin. She still seemed to be in her late thirties. By all accounts, she should be in her late fifties now, at the very least. Most women her age would have the signs of time around their eyes, yet she didn't have one.

"Yes, we are." She shook her head and touched my arm briefly. "Do you want a drink, Hugh?"

"Sure," I stated as she began to step away. I paused midstep, wondering if I was safe here, and she twirled around, lifting a brow, and then laughed again as she approached me.

"Don't worry, you're safe here, Hugh." She put her hand on my chest, over my heart, and I wondered if she could feel it thudding against my breastbone. "I know there are many stories out there about us, but they aren't all true, and most of us don't act the way you see in the news."

"Ah," I replied. I stood, unable to move as her hand caressed my chest, drifted over my tense stomach, and then dropped away. Holy fuck—was Bridgette hitting on me?

"Come on, Hugh, let's go back to the kitchen."

I tried not to watch the sway of her hips as she went, but it was damn hard not to after the way she had just touched me. "Is Henry here?"

"No, he's at work." She peered seductively over her shoulder. "As you can assume, he works nights."

Jesus, the thoughts that were running through my mind with the knowledge that her husband wasn't home were making me a bit hot under the collar. Especially as I looked at the height of her counters and realized they would be perfect. I heard a soft chuckle, and I quickly cleared my throat and pulled out a chair. I needed to get my head back into business, and not that head.

"Can you go into the sunlight?" I blurted out the question as I took a seat at her table.

Nice change of subject. I forced myself not to frown as the soft voice slipped through my mind. My subconscious had turned female, weird.

Bridgette began to talk and gathered my attention. "Some of the young ones can, the older you get, the more dangerous it becomes."

"How old do you get?"

She laughed as she took two beers out of the fridge and held one up. I nodded, and she closed the refrigerator. "We can get very old."

"Are we talking a hundred years, five hundred?"

"There are many of us out there that are well over the hundred-year mark. You earn the elder title when you hit five hundred."

"Elders?" I asked.

She took a seat across me at the end of the table and handed me the bottle. Our fingers touched briefly, and my dick twitched. "Yes, elders."

"Who are the elders?"

She studied me. "Hugh, you do know that I am aware of what you do for the government. Although I'm not sure what the purpose of this special task force is. As much as I'd like to share information with you, I'm not at liberty to say much, although if you'd like to share anything with me, I'd be happy to enjoy it."

Did she think I had information to share with her? Maybe if I told her about the task force, she might share more.

Or maybe you could just fuck me, and I'd share a thing or two with you.

CHAPTER THREE

HUGH

*T*he bottle froze at my lips, and I stared at her. Her full sexy lips spread into a wide smile. "What do you say, Hugh?" She slipped her foot up the side of my leg, inching it toward my suddenly hard crotch.

"Did you just talk to me mentally?" I set the bottle down with a slight shake in my hands. I shifted in my seat and grabbed hold of her foot right before it hit the bullseye.

She practically giggled. "No." She hiked a manicured brow as I frowned. "But I can think of a few things I'd like to whisper into your ear while I did other things to your body."

Jesus. H. Christ—my dick was instantly throbbing, and I glanced toward the counter, swallowing as I easily pictured her sitting there with her long legs wrapped around my hips.

A wicked smile crossed her lips. "It would be the perfect height."

My eyes slammed closed, and I forced myself to stay seated and not lunge toward her. It had been a while since I'd been with a woman, and the one in front of me was sinful as fuck— but she was married, and she was a vampire. Did they have sex the same way? The thought of her biting me while I was deep inside of her almost made me moan, and I fought a shiver.

"As incredible as I'm sure that would be, I don't sleep with married women."

"He wouldn't mind. In fact, Henry would probably want to watch or even join in if you were up for it."

I pushed my chair back with a screech. Not far, just far enough that her foot fell to the floor. "I take it your husband is not a jealous man?"

"No, he is not, and we don't view relationships as humans do. Monogamy is not the same with our kind."

"As tempting as that might be, Bridgette, it's probably not a good idea."

She sighed and gave me a saucy look. "Fine, but if you change your mind, you just let me know." She grew quiet for a moment, and her forehead creased slightly. "While my husband wouldn't care if I had sex with you, he would probably be upset that I have said anything to you."

"Bridgette, I'm not out to hurt you or anyone else like you. Our task force is trying to learn about your species so that we can help *you*. We'd also like to stop the violence."

"Well, the violence has been coming for a long time."

"Why did the vampires show themselves after all these years?"

She wrapped her hand around her bottle and stared at it for a few seconds before lifting her pretty brown eyes to me. "Hugh, there is a war coming between two sides of our kind. One side has always wished to remain in the shadows, the other wishes to take over the world. The war is building, and it will only be a matter of time before it comes to a head and things get very bloody."

I tensed. "What can I do to stop that?"

Her features grew intense, and she suddenly looked like a

formidable opponent and not the sexy siren she had a few moments ago. "Stay out of it. I know that you only want to protect your humans, but the more of you that get involved, the more of you that will get hurt. It would be better if you all looked the other way for a time."

"That's not an option, Bridgette."

"I'm sure that you think it's not, but it is what you should convince your people to do."

"How soon will this war take place?"

She shrugged. "It will happen soon, not sure if you'll still be working when it does."

I frowned at her. "What does that mean?"

"Soon for us is much different than soon for you. It could be next year, or it could be ten years from now. You might be retired by then." She smiled brightly at me. "In which case, it won't matter to you anyway."

I laughed softly and took a drink. "Who decides if there will be a war?"

She studied me. "You have a million questions in your mind right now, Hugh, but I can't answer them all—unless you want to give me something in return."

"What? Sex? You're saying that if I have sex with you, you'd tell me more?"

"You say that like there is something wrong with it. I would get what I want, and you would get what you want and then some."

"Bridgette—" I started to say.

"Listen, Hugh." She spoke in an ultra-sexy voice as she leaned back in her seat, lifting her skirt and spreading her legs. My partially deflated erection exploded back into its aroused state. "Get on your knees, Hugh."

I clenched my teeth, wanting to fight it but strangely unable to as I began to slip off the chair and to my knees. My hands immediately spread wide over Bridgette's thighs and pushed her skirt the rest of the way up. She was shaved bare, and I almost whimpered at the sight.

"How long do you live?" I asked her gruffly as I tried to force myself off my knees. This was so wrong, but goddamn, the sight in front of me was glorious.

"Forever if we aren't killed. Lick me, Hugh." She said the words huskily, and I felt like I had no choice, bending to her and spreading her wide. Her lilac scent even more potent now as I got lost in the taste of her.

I lifted back after a few moments, stroking her with two fingers and pushing them in as I asked, "Do you kill humans?"

Her head tipped back. "Most of us, oh god—don't hurt humans—yes—harder! We only take their blood for pleasure, or because we need it." She sat up quickly, one moment in front of me, the next on the counter a few feet away.

I stared in surprise at her. "Yes, we can move fast." She crooked a finger toward me, and once again, I moved as if I had no choice. As I reached her, she leaned forward and undid my belt and zipper in record time. I stared at my erection, and she curled her legs around my back and pulled me forward. I watched my flesh disappear into hers, and I sucked in a deep breath at the feeling. This wasn't why I had come here. I'd come to ask questions, and yet, I was screwing this beautiful woman —vampire—what the fuck! It was like my muscles had a mind of their own.

She pulled one of my hands to her chest, between her breasts, and I felt it just as she spoke. "Our hearts beat, we fall in love, we have children." She rolled her hips. "Move, Hugh."

I began to move within her, pushing in and then slowly pulling back out.

"We enjoy eating all kinds of food." She hissed as I slammed into her harder. My body had its own agenda as I listened to her speak. "We do all the normal things that you do: watch movies, shop, work, pay bills, go out to dinner." Her hand went between her legs, and I watched as she pleasured herself. The urge to hit my climax was rising quickly, and I began to move faster. "We are no different, except we are stronger, we love harder, and we live longer."

The two of us hit the pinnacle at the same time, Bridgette's final words coming out stuttered as I slammed into her with everything that I had. For a few moments, we were both quiet. I was both physically satisfied and mentally horrified at myself.

She lifted her head to me and smiled as I forced myself to continue with questions. "Who is this war going to be between —your race and ours?"

She shook her head and shifted her hips to dislodge our bodies. "I'd hate to see that; it would get gruesome. The war that I am talking about is within our race. Hence the reason I told you to stay out of it." She hopped off the counter, and I quickly shoved myself back inside my pants and zipped them up.

"What is it about?" I asked her as I followed her back to the table.

"What is any war about? Power and control, of course."

In the back part of my mind, I was astounded that I'd just had sex with Bridgette. Did we really have sex while I quizzed her over her kind? Had I imagined that? I turned and looked back at the counter. "Do you all have a government?"

She was smirking as I turned back around. "That was very real, Hugh, and thank you, by the way. It was just what I needed. We have something similar to what you'd call a government."

I pursed my lips. "Why did we just have sex?"

"Because I wanted to have sex with you, and you wanted to know these answers."

I stared at her, knowing that I wouldn't usually trade sex for answers with anyone. Why was she different?

She shook her head, her dark hair swishing back and forth

over her shoulders. "Sorry, there are some things that I cannot share."

"Did you do something to me?" I glared at her.

"Yes, I gave you an incredible orgasm." She grinned.

"Who is in charge of your government?"

"Sorry, Hugh." She gulped her beer. "That is another thing I can't share with you."

"Why? Why would it be so bad for us to know who is in charge of your race?"

"Breed. We call it a breed."

"Okay, your breed. Why can't we know who is in charge? Wouldn't that make sense for us to speak with them and see if we can help rectify the situation?"

She gave me a stern look, all sexy teasing gone. "It could get me killed, Hugh. It could get you killed. Why do you think we have stayed quiet this long?"

"I don't know—why—how?"

"Because we knew that one day, we would have to deal with this. There have been a few incidents in history where our existence almost came out in the open, but each time we were able to shield it from humans."

"Why did it come out now?"

"Because someone wants you all to know that you are on the lower spectrum of our food chain."

"You said that you don't normally feed on humans."

"Well, many do. I mean, we do feed on people, but we don't kill them. Normally, when we feed on humans, we have sex with them, too."

I tensed; had she fed on me?

She laughed and patted my chest. "Relax, Hugh, I did not take your vein. Trust me; if I did, you would have known. That orgasm would have been twice as good." She winked.

"I'm trusting you on that," I muttered. "So these other people think we are the lower spectrum? Do they want to control us?"

She nodded.

"Is that what you want?"

"Oh, no. I am all for co-existence between humans and our breed. As you can see, I happen to like humans. I'm on the side that wishes you all were still in the dark."

"Can you at least tell me who the person or group is that wants it another way? Maybe we can focus our attention on them and stop the war before it starts."

She sighed. "Hugh, there is nothing that you can do to stop it. Like I said earlier, it would be best if you stayed out of it."

"Yeah, well, I guess you know that's not going to happen, Bridgette."

She smiled sadly. "Yes, I do. I can only hope you all survive it when it does happen."

A few minutes later, it was apparent that Bridgette was finished talking, and she showed me to the door. I was just arriving back at my transport when I glanced at her house, an uneasy feeling slipping down my spine.

I had never done anything unethical in my life to get answers, and I sure as hell hadn't had any intention of having sex with Bridgette when I had gone to her house. How had that happened? It was almost like my dick had a mind of its own.

I sank into my seat and started the transport. Had Bridgette done something to me? Had she been able to influence me into having sex with her? She had to have. There was no other way I would have done that. Was that considered rape? Even if quite honestly, my body had been more than willing? Fuck, if I knew, and I wasn't sure I could ask anyone.

I pulled down the street and then put the transport back into park, running my hands over my face. I'd just had sex with a vampire. I wasn't even sure what to do with that knowledge.

What I did know was that I had some general information now, and at least I could start working off that. Maybe Bridgette would talk to me again later. Or perhaps that was my dick still talking and wondering when we were going to have another round.

I growled to myself and put the transport back into drive, telling it where to go so I could start recording notes into my recorder on the way to the office.

CHAPTER FOUR

HUGH

I had been leading the V-Force for over almost seven months now with Tom Singer, and we currently had a listing of over six thousand confirmed vampires that resided in the U.S., although we were aware of thousands more living around the globe. Some we had quite a bit of information on, others we did not.

The information I had initially acquired from Bridgette had helped us set up a game plan, and I'd gone back to her twice for more. Each time, I questioned her before, during, and after the hot sex. She might have influenced my mind the first time, but I had been an eager participant in the next two.

Our technology department had gotten their hands on some of their weapons, and we had realized that they used unique bullets with a special kind of alloy combination that could reduce the strength of a vampire drastically. We now had a supply of ammunition and handcuffs made from these materials, and all of us carried them.

We'd taken a few vampires into custody during our investigation, and of course, most refused to speak with us. A few gave us the runaround, but for the most part, none of them would answer the questions that we needed responses for—not until today.

Today, we had a young human male in his twenties in our interview room. He wasn't detained for questioning because he had done something. No, he had walked into our doors on his own accord to share information that he had learned.

"Is there anything else that I can get for you, Ted?" I asked as he finished eating the sandwich that I'd brought in for him.

He shook his head, his cheeks gaunt, his face shadowed by more than stubble. This man looked like he had seen war. "No, this is enough, thank you."

"When is the last time that you ate?"

"Um, they usually fed me every morning, not much, but enough to give me energy and still keep making blood."

"How long were you with them?"

"With them, the group you mean?" I nodded, "Um, maybe a month or so. I don't remember. The days kind of rolled into one another after a while."

"How did you get involved with them?"

"I was only involved with one of them, a girl. I met Trina at a club. She told me what she was, said she wanted to give me the best sex of my life."

"The best sex of your life?" I thought back on Bridgette. It had been pretty good, but I wasn't sure it was the best sex of my life.

He grinned, his eyes almost brightening. "Yeah, and it was. When they have sex, that's when they like to feed. When Trina bit into my neck, it was like I wanted to explode, but not in a bad way. It was kind of incredible, the best thing I had ever felt really. Better than any drug out there on the market; that's for sure."

So that's why sex with Bridgette wasn't the best sex of my life. She hadn't fed from me. "Okay, so you had the best sex of your life with Trina. How long were you with her?"

"Maybe six months. We were a couple. I really liked her." His shoulders rounded as he sank lower in his chair. "I guess you could say I loved her. Is that weird that I was in love with a vampire?"

"We can't help who we love, Ted. Did she love you back?" I asked.

"Yeah, she did. That's what was wrong. A few of her friends started pushing her to get rid of me, but she didn't want to. She told me that she wanted to turn me."

I stared at him, my mind jumping in a dozen directions, and I fought hard to make my next question nonchalant. "They can turn humans?"

"Yeah, they can, although it's against their laws to do so. Trina told me that if she did do it, the VMF might kill us both, but I might have a better chance of living since I was a male."

"The VMF? What is that?"

He shook his head. "I don't know what the letters stand for, but it's like their police, I guess. She said that when someone does something wrong, they come down on them. A lot of the time, they are killed for doing something illegal."

I was trying hard to keep my cool because this was the first time that we had solid confirmation on the fact that they had people overseeing laws. We knew that they must have, but this information confirmed that. When I didn't speak, he continued.

"Trina said it was too dangerous to do it around here, but she said that she had heard of a place in Kentucky where they could help us out. That we could be together forever, and I could be like her."

"Do you know where in Kentucky?"

He shook his head again. "No. She only said Kentucky."

"Okay, so you two were going to go to Kentucky, and she was going to turn you. Did she ever tell you how that would happen?"

"She told me that she'd have to drain me of my blood and

then give me some of hers before she killed me. After that, I'd wake up like her."

"Did she tell you anything else about it?"

"Only that she hated having to do it. She was scared that it wouldn't work. She didn't want to kill me; she's not a violent person. Most of them aren't, at least the ones that I've met before. If they were ever violent, it was to protect themselves. She was afraid she would do something wrong, and I'd be dead for good."

"Did you want her to change you?"

"Hell, yeah. I told you I loved Trina. I would have done anything for her."

"Why didn't you two do it then?"

He sighed and rubbed his hands over his face. "Because I guess she talked to the wrong person about it. Trina came home to our apartment about a month ago and was scared and upset, but she wouldn't tell me why. A few minutes after she showed up, three guys busted in the door and took us both."

"Where did they take you?"

"I didn't know then. They put something over my head, but I knew they were vampires. They were too strong. I couldn't fight them; she tried, but they overpowered her, too. Of course, I have since learned I was in a warehouse in the south end of town."

"What happened after they took you?"

"They took us to this warehouse and stuck me in a room. I didn't know where Trina was or what they were doing to her. A few hours after we arrived, they brought her into me and threw her at my feet; she was badly beaten, almost dead. I fed her some of my blood, and she started to heal, but then they came back and took her away again. When they did, one of the guys stayed in the room with me."

His voice dropped, and so did his eyes as he shifted in his chair. "What happened then, Ted?"

He was quiet for a long time, and when he spoke, his voice shook. "The guy wanted to know why she was so fascinated with me. He thought maybe I had some magical blood, and he bit me." He paused and closed his eyes, his voice dropping to a whisper. "Then he raped me while he fed from my neck."

I clenched my jaw and forced myself not to clench my hands on the table.

A tear slipped down his cheek. "The thing is, because of the way it feels when they put their teeth in you, you don't care if it's a man or a woman who is touching you. You just feel incredible, and all you want to do is get off."

He opened his eyes and stared at me. I knew he was wondering if I would think differently of him, but I didn't. He was a victim, a survivor in my mind, and he deserved my compassion and respect.

"I'm sorry for what they did."

He nodded and looked away, sniffling and swiping at his cheek. "After, I felt terrible—almost guilty because I had enjoyed it while at the same time hated it. My body hurt, and I was weak, and I curled up and slept. I think it was the next day when Trina's body was left in my room. She was dead." His voice sounded hollow. "They kept me around for a few weeks, feeding me in the morning, taking my blood at night. Almost every night, someone would come to me and drink from me, and most times, have sex with me. It wasn't always men, sometimes women too. A few times, there were multiple people. After that first time, I tried to fight, but as soon as they bit me, I stopped fighting and was powerless to do anything else but go with it."

I closed my eyes and exhaled loudly. "Jesus, Ted, I'm so sorry."

He nodded mutely.

"I'm sorry about Trina, too."

Another tear slipped down his cheek as he glanced around the room. "That's why I came here. I knew that I needed to tell someone. They might kill me for saying something, but at least if they do, I won't have to relive it all in my head forever."

"Do you remember everything that they did to you?"

He nodded slowly, his light-green eyes wide and bloodshot as he stared at me. "Every single raw second."

"Do you remember anything else that you heard or that Trina told you about the breed?"

"I know she said that a woman, they call her the mistress, was in charge of the VMF, but it was a guy named Portage that would have helped her turn me."

"Portage?"

"Yeah, he's the one that's supposed to be in Kentucky. I guess he helps people turn, and he protects them."

"Do you know who the mistress is?"

He shook his head. "No, Trina always called her the mistress."

"What did she say about her?"

"Not much." He sighed. "Just that she was extremely power-ful, and that she, Trina, had always believed in what she stood for, except for turning people. Trina thought that we should be able to make up our minds on that. She thought the law was stupid."

"The mistress is the one that doesn't allow humans to be turned? Do you know why?"

"No, Trina wouldn't explain it to me. Even though we were together for a while, she was cautious not to say too much. She said it would be dangerous for me to know until I was one of them."

"How did you get free?"

He shrugged. "I don't know. I was in my room for two days; no one came to feed me or feed on me. Finally, I tried the door and found out it was unlocked. When I opened the door, the place was quiet, and no one was around. I walked right out and found the first police officer I could and told him to get me to whoever deals with vampire crimes."

"Ted, you were very brave to come here. We're going to put you someplace safe for a while. Would that be okay?"

"Yeah, that will be fine, but I need to call my parents and tell them that I am okay."

"We will let you make a phone call, but it might be better if you don't see them right now." I tapped my fingers on the table for a moment. "Is there anything else you can tell me about the mistress or this Portage guy?"

"I know that the mistress wants to protect the breed and humans. I'm pretty sure Portage wants to wipe the humans out of existence; that's why he was willing to turn me."

THREE HOURS LATER, I was staring at an enormous virtual computer screen that took up the whole wall of one room. Displayed were notes about what we had gathered over our course of the investigation. At the top of each corner were two bold words: on the left, Mistress, and the right, Portage.

Our tech department was already running information to see what we could come up with on those two people, but there was very little. I stared between the two words, determined to figure it all out. It might take my entire lifetime, but I would do it.

CHAPTER FIVE

HUGH

*I*t was the beginning of March, and at the start of every month, we all went out for drinks to celebrate any upcoming birthdays. At the very end of next month, I would celebrate mine. I never wanted to make a big deal about my birthday, especially this year. Turning forty was putting me more on edge than any birthday before ever had. My co-workers held up glasses and offered toasts to a few people who were celebrating this month, and I tried to get in the party mood, but I couldn't.

The reminder that this time next month I'd be accepting those wishes and jokes about hitting forty was not something I was looking forward to. For the last few months, I felt like I had a bomb equipped with a countdown timer inside my chest. Both my father and his father had died when they were forty, and that weighed heavily on my mind.

So much so that just a few weeks ago, I had gone to the doctor to get a physical. I had told the doc that I wanted a full workup. The last thing I wanted them to do was miss something that could have been caught ahead of time. Earlier today, I'd received a phone call from my doctor saying that everything looked perfect, and he'd see me next year. As I hung up the phone, I wondered if I'd still be alive then.

"Hey." Bruce slapped me on the back. "Cheer up. You look like you're turning forty already."

I laughed. "I still have a month, but it will be here before I know it."

"Yeah, well, I only have a couple more years until I retire, so think about that."

"You're not going to retire, are you?"

He shrugged. "Yeah, why not. I'm tired of all this mess. I want to hit a beach someplace and be shit-faced all day while I make love to beautiful women all night."

I grinned. "I can just imagine you doing that, too."

His tone changed, and he grew serious. "You really enjoy working on the V-Force, don't you?"

"I do. It's interesting, and we've learned a lot over the last year."

"Yeah, did you figure out how to stop the two sides from killing all the people stuck in the middle?"

"I wish." I tossed back my drink. "We know more about them, but damn if they don't keep those in power hidden behind tightly locked doors. Both of them are like ghosts. Sometimes I feel like people want to talk about them, but physically can't. It doesn't make sense."

"I heard that one of them was a woman, a beautiful woman with long red hair."

"The mistress, yeah, that's about all we have on her; we have heard that she is young too, but I have no idea what young means because they track time different than we do. She could be two hundred and not five hundred—who the fuck knows." He had just brought up a tense subject for me, and I kept on rolling. "We have no idea where she lives or works, although there are rumors she is in the northeast someplace. One person said Boston, another said Poughkeepsie, New York, someone else said she's right here in Philly. No one can give us a straight answer. We also don't know what she does other than track down members of her breed that are breaking laws and exterminating them."

He laughed. "You mean, she just executes them?"

"Pretty much, at least that's what we believe or have been told. I'm pretty sure the mistress herself doesn't do it, but she has her underlings carry out the task." I laughed. "Who knows she might be the one that does it herself for the fun of it."

"What about the other guy? What's his deal?"

"Damn, Bruce, we know even less about him. No one speaks about him—like ever. At least with the mistress, they say the same stuff—she's beautiful and sexy. That kid I interviewed months ago, well, he's the only one that has ever even spoken the guy's name. People say there is a man who wants control, but no one will even mutter his goddamn name."

"That's really strange. You would think that someone would know something."

"That is what you would think." I stood up with a sigh and slapped him on the back. "I'm gonna head out; I have an early morning."

"I'll walk you out. I have to catch a plane in the morning myself and head down to Georgia. We have a cell that is starting to make waves, and we heard something about bombs at the state capitol there."

As Bruce and I hit the sidewalk, I pulled my coat a little tighter as a cold blast of air whipped around us. We turned to walk toward the parking garage where our transports were parked and chatted about bullshit on the way. Bruce slapped me on the back and wished me well as we split up in the garage.

I was almost to my transport when someone spoke behind me. I spun around, my hand going to my hip where my gun was. The man was standing behind me dressed in black leather and wearing a mask over his face. His shoulders were broad, like linebacker wide, and his eyes were a vivid green that seemed almost unreal. A second man dressed the same way was off to his left. "Hugh McMurphy?"

I figured if they wanted to hurt me, they would have done it when I hadn't known they were there. "Yeah, who wants to know?"

"We'd like you to come with us."

"For what reason?"

"Someone wants to speak with you."

"Who?"

"Someone you might be interested in speaking with."

Could the guy be any more cryptic? "Look, if someone wants to speak to me, they can come to find me themselves."

His green eyes darkened, and a muscle ticked in his jaw. "We can do this the easy way or the hard way, Agent McMurphy, but you will be coming with us."

As I stared back at the guy, I suddenly realized that this might be a good thing. If someone in higher power wanted to speak with me, it wasn't surprising that they used muscle to do their bidding.

"Fine, I'll come with you because I'm intrigued and for no other reason," I stated gruffly.

He grinned at me. "Wise choice." He turned and held his hand out. "Right this way, Agent McMurphy."

I moved toward a large black transport that he motioned to, and as I reached the back door, an arm wrapped around my neck, panic exploded from my gut, and then I felt a pinch. A moment later, the world around me disappeared.

When I woke up, my head was banging. It was like having that hangover that so many people talked about, but I had never experienced it. A groan left my lips as I tried to move and realized I was lying down. My eyes snapped open as the memory slammed into my mind of how I had gotten here.

"Relax, Agent McMurphy." A deep voice spoke from off to the side. "You are safe, and no harm will come to you here."

I surged upright and scanned the area to find an older man off to the side, looking at a piece of paper. Was he a human or a vampire? I had a feeling he wasn't human, and he appeared to be in his forties, which meant that if he were a vampire, he must be old. Was he one of the elders that I had heard mentioned?

"Who are you and why the hell am I here?"

"Well, as for why you are here, I heard you have been looking for me, Agent McMurphy. I thought it was time to make an introduction."

"Most people who hear I'd like to talk to them come to me in person; they don't send goons to drug and kidnap me."

"Agent McMurphy." He paused as he set the paper down and began to approach. "May I call you Hugh?"

"You can call me whatever you want as long as you explain what the hell is going on. Kidnapping a federal agent doesn't go over very well."

He smiled, a look that might put many at ease, but did the opposite to me. "Your kidnapping is only temporary. Don't worry; you will be returned shortly to your life. My name is Joseph Portage."

I forced myself not to react visually, although my heart sped up some as he took a seat across from me in a leather wingback chair. "Alright, so you're Portage. Why did you want to see me?"

"As I said, I heard you were looking for me."

I thought about that for a second. I could play it cool and pretend like I didn't know what Portage was talking about, or I could jump in and get as much as I could out of the man.

I felt like taking a swim. "Yes, I was. I hear you and the mistress are fighting."

"Ah, the illustrious mistress. What do you know about her?"

"Honestly?"

He smirked. "Yes, I'd prefer that."

"About as much as I know about you. I know that you both have different viewpoints on how your breed should survive. The mistress wants to live in peace; you want to wage war."

"It's not that I *want* to wage war, Hugh. It's that I want what is rightfully mine."

"Which is?"

"To be the master. She has no rights to the position. It is I who should be ruling our race."

"Why do you think that?"

"Because I am the rightful heir. I should have held the position before the former master was in place."

"The former master? Who was that? How often do you all go through masters?"

"Usually not often, and his name was Alexander Armstrong." He grinned.

"So you want to oust the current mistress and take over the breed. Is that all you want to do?"

"Of course not. I want to command the breed. Bring our people to where they should be and make humans kneel to our superiority."

I laughed. "You think you're superior to humans?"

"I don't think, Hugh. I know."

I leaned back on the couch, pretending to be at ease. "Why do you think you are better than us?"

"Us?" He laughed. "Hugh, you aren't one of them."

I frowned. "What the hell are you talking about?"

He smirked and then chuckled slightly. "There is much you do not know, and I promise to bring you up to speed."

"Start talking, Portage. What did you mean I wasn't one of them?"

"You, Hugh, are not human at all. You are one of us. A rare version of our kind."

I stared at him for a long moment and then began to laugh. "Are you crazy? I'm as human as you can get."

"Oh, but that's not true." He reached into a small chest on the table beside him and pulled out a cigar. He held it up to me, and I shook my head. "Cuban, you don't know what you're missing."

"I'll take my chances."

He messed with the cigar for a moment, and I wondered if he was doing that to make me uneasy. Finally, he got it lit and blew smoke up toward the ceiling. "They won't kill us. I've been smoking them for two hundred years."

"That's nice; now what were you saying about me?"

"Ah, yes, you were raised by humans, but you are far from that. You are what we call a reborn."

"A what?"

"A reborn. Someone in your family was previously a full-blooded member of our society. They died, and their soul was reborn into yours."

"That makes absolutely no fucking sense, and how the hell would you even know that?"

"Did you not see your doctor recently?"

I glared at him. "What does that have to do with anything?"

"You saw your doctor because you were concerned that you are nearing your fortieth birthday, and both your father and grandfather died at that age. You were being smart, went in for a full physical, even had blood tests done."

"Yeah, so."

"Well, those blood tests confirmed that you are indeed one of us. Welcome to the family." He grinned before he took another puff of his cigar.

This guy was a lunatic. "How the fuck would you know about my tests?"

"I have many people on my payroll, Hugh. They watch for certain things, and when they find what I am looking for, they let me know." He let that settle over me before he continued. "Most humans have forty-six chromosomes, occasionally a male will have forty-seven, but not often. Vampires have forty-eight, twenty-four pairs, but you, Hugh. You have twenty-five pairs. Only reborn vampires have fifty chromosomes."

"What are you saying? I'm a vampire?" This guy really was psychotic.

"You could be if you so choose to be."

I laughed and shifted on the couch. If I chose to be? "Why did you want to talk to me? Why was it important for you to tell me this? Why couldn't my doctor have told me?"

"Well, yes. I did want to tell you about this, but I also wanted to help you, Hugh."

"Help me? With what? You want to drain me of my blood, kill me, and then turn me into a vampire?" I didn't want to fear this man, but the feeling was slowly starting to grow deep inside of me.

He shook his head. "Oh, no, turning you would be quite different. That is how mere humans are turned. Remember, you're not human."

"I am very human," I growled toward him.

He sighed. "Hugh, you are not human. You are one of us, and you will be an essential person in our world. Reborn vampires are rare and strong. Many possess special abilities. Wouldn't you want that? Wouldn't you want to be immortal and do things that you can only dream about now? You could be at my side, at the top, helping me rule."

I laughed uneasily. "I'm not sure about that." For a moment, I glanced anywhere but at him, focusing instead on his room. The walls were all wood with large beams along the ceiling, like a log cabin—the furniture sturdy.

"You are meant to be more than you are, Hugh. I can help you achieve that."

I turned my attention back to him. "Let's say that for just one minute I believe your fucked-up story; why would you want to help me?"

"Because I believe that everyone has the right to what they

are entitled to have or be. You deserve to live your true nature; you deserve to become one of us. You are so much more than what you think you are."

"Why should I believe you?"

"Because I can give it all to you, Hugh. I can help you gain your rightful place in this world."

"And what would you want in return?"

"I'd want you to help me take the mistress down, of course." His words were so pleasant, as if he'd asked for sugar in his tea and not for me to kill someone.

A burst of laughter spilled from my mouth. "You want me to kill the mistress? I don't even know who the hell she is, and I don't go around killing people to further my interests."

He inhaled sharply and then released it slowly. "Well, then I guess I will have to do this the hard way."

Suddenly, my survival instincts began to kick in, and I tensed. Was he going to kill me now? Try to turn me into a vampire? He took another long drag on his cigar and then blew it out before he shifted in his seat and stared at me hard, his brown eyes moving to a lighter shade as he began to speak.

"You will do as I ask, Hugh. You will not *want* to ask me any questions. Do you understand that?"

"Yes," I replied.

I blinked, and then blinked again. The white ceiling above me so in contrast to the dream that I had just had. I turned and looked at the window; the sun was shining behind the curtains. What had happened to the log cabin? I swear I was in a log cabin. I sniffed the air and then my shirt. I could just make out the scent of cigar smoke in the fabric. What the fuck?

Had it all been a dream? It must have been, but it couldn't be if my shirt smelled like smoke. I sat up, my head banging like it never had before. Holy shit, what the fuck did I drink last night? Had I gone somewhere else after I left the bar with my co-workers? Had I been around someone smoking a cigar?

I rubbed my eyes with the heels of my hands as a name I'd never heard before slipped through my mind: Kristin Armstrong. Kristin Armstrong. I glanced back at the bed; had I brought someone home with me? The other side of the bed was smooth as if it hadn't been slept in.

Who was Kristin Armstrong? My head pounded, and then another word appeared in my mind: mistress.

CHAPTER SIX

JOSEPH

"You have a call from a Doctor Dewell," Melinda said as she poked her head into my study.

"Thank you," I told her and moved to my desk to answer it. "This is Portage."

"Mr. Portage, this is Dr. Dewell. I believe that you had requested me to reach out to you if I ever ran across a similar test result like the one that you had supplied for me before."

"Yes, does this mean that you have?"

"Yes, I believe so. The patient came in for a checkup and requested a full workup be done on him. His blood tests came back, and he has fifty chromosomes, exactly like the results that you showed me before. It's fascinating! How did you know that there would be someone like him?"

"I've heard of such people before." I started to grin. "And who is this person?"

"I'm sorry, Mr. Portage, you know I can't give you patient names."

I laughed. "Of course you can, Dr. Dewell. In fact, you *want* to give me everything that you have," I stressed in my compelling voice. It made life so easy to be able to get people to do what you wanted all the time—the perfect thing for a master to be able to achieve.

"Oh, yes, you're right. I did want you to know. The patient's name is Hugh McMurphy."

McMurphy? I don't recall any McMurphys in our world. "How old is he?"

"Almost forty, sir." Ah, so he's getting close to the end of his life. Made sense that he would want a full workup if he had some strange inkling of what would be coming for him soon.

"And what does he do?"

I heard buttons tapping on a keyboard. "It seems he works for the Department of Homeland Security, sir."

I chuckled to myself, although I wanted to jump up and click my heels together in glee. I couldn't have planned this any better. "That is great, Doc. I appreciate you calling and letting me know. Now, you *want* to send me his entire file. Everything that you have on this man, and then after you do that, I *want* you to forget that we have spoken about this matter. Do you understand me, Dr. Dewell?"

"Yes, sir. I'll send this information over to you now."

"Thank you, Doctor."

"You're welcome, Mr. Portage."

The phone line went dead. I sat in my seat for a few minutes, staring at the virtual screen and waiting for the information to come into my inbox. The moment it did, I opened it and grinned as I got a look at his picture.

"My patience has paid off in spades," I said as I stared at the handsome man on the screen. No doubt, Hugh McMurphy was attractive enough that he would get her attention. I enlarged the image and stared at his eyes—fucking perfect! I wondered how long it would take her to figure out that he was a reborn.

I read over his entire file, and I paused as I got to his kin. Of course, I had known Galen, his great-grandfather. He had been too kind for my liking. He preferred to enjoy life rather than control it, and it had killed him on a fishing boat—his loss, my gain.

I picked up my cellphone and dialed a number. "Adam, I need you to track someone for me. You might need to get one of our human volunteers to work on this too since the guy has a day job, but I need to know everything about him."

"Yes, sir, send me over the information."

* * *

FOUR DAYS LATER, Adam delivered Hugh McMurphy to me practically tied with a ribbon. He was everything I had hoped for and more. His job would give him advantages, and his mental capabilities would work well for him. His mind turned over questions, and he pushed the ones that weren't important out of the way to make room for those that would give him more information. I also noticed that he tried to hide his questions occasionally, and I knew that he could only do that if someone had taught him. Interesting.

I had hoped that I could get his assistance by promising him power, but unfortunately, he was a man of integrity, and I had no room in my life for such nonsense. Later he could show me his integrity and honor.

"You will *want* to find a way to meet the mistress, Hugh. When you meet her, you will *want* and desire her, above all reason. You will do anything to stay in her good graces. You will *want* the mistress to become a friend. You will *want* to be her lover, and you will let her know that you want her. She will want you back because she will feel something in you that she doesn't understand. You will take her, sleep with her, get her to trust you, care about you. You will *want* to show her passion, love, and understanding. You will *want* to make her happy, and you will *want* to be with her as often as you can. Once you are close to her, and she has accepted you into her life, you will *want* to contact me again."

I stared at Hugh as my commands filtered into his mind and were absorbed.

"Remember, you will *want* to desire her, you will *want* to be with her, do anything for her, maybe you will even *want* to fall in love with her, and then you will contact me when she wants you as much. Do you understand that, Hugh?"

"Yes."

I grinned. "Good, now you will *want* to sleep through the day and be brought home tomorrow night. You will *want* to forget this conversation or meeting me. You will only *want* to remember being out with your friends for the evening; your loss of memory and missing work will be chalked up to having too much to drink. You will *want* to remember one name, Kristin Armstrong. She is the mistress that you will need to find. She lives in the Philadelphia First Regency Hotel. You will *want* to remember that, but you will not want to remember me. You will *want* to call me on this number when you have done what is needed, and only then. Do you understand this?"

"Yes, I understand."

I gave him the phone number and then told him to sleep.

Adam took him to the guest room to sleep, and then the next evening, Adam took him home to Philadelphia. After Adam called and told me Hugh had been returned to his apartment, I kicked my feet up on my desk and grinned. I had been waiting for this type of opportunity for so long, and it was finally here.

For many years, I had had vampires tested to see if I could find the genes for a reborn. I knew they were different—my son carried them—but I needed someone else. Zander was too special for this first part. After figuring out what I was looking for, I started working on doctors and labs to find someone else who might come forward that we didn't yet know about. I had learned of a few, but they didn't fit the bill for what I needed.

The last six that had been located were killed immediately. I didn't want any more reborns out there than needed to be.

My goal was to infiltrate the mistress' world and take over from inside. If this worked, within a year or so, she would either be dead or mated to me. The thought of having her at my side excited me, but the idea of finally being in my rightful place gave me a raging hard-on.

IT WAS several weeks later when I received the call from Hugh. I had people observing him, and I had even made sure that some helpful information was passed along so that he could acquire a meeting with the mistress. Of course, he thought it was for his own silly human world need. I didn't care what excuse he used as long as he made contact.

When Hugh called me and told me that he had not only been transitioned but that he was now mated to Kristin, I knew that my plan was right on track. I had expected them to accept him, turn him, but I could never have hoped that someone close to her would have turned him or that he would mate with her.

For a moment, I wondered if this had been the right thing to do. What would happen with two reborns mated to one another? I had to believe that my compulsion would remain as reliable as it had been. Maybe, I needed to bring him back for a refresher and see if he was still on my side. If he were, I'd give him some time to learn our ways, get more involved with her, see what I could learn, and then I would tear her fucking world apart.

CHAPTER SEVEN

KRISTIN

To say that I was nervous about mating with Hugh was an understatement. There was very little that made me question myself, but this decision did. I was about to have a man that I didn't know transition and mate to me. My mind warred with this; my heart balked at it, but the inherent part of me that I had always trusted told me this was the right thing to do.

I pondered the fact that if you considered my history, I made a habit out of mating men that I didn't know. I hadn't known Julian or Trent, but I had loved them both.

Julian and I had mated because of the chemistry between us the night after we met. We never talked about it, weighed the pros and cons. We listened to our hearts and became one without a word. The chemistry between us was always so intense, so consuming. For a second, my chest ached, and I closed my eyes and inhaled slowly.

Was I mating with Hugh because he had Julian's eyes? There was nothing else about him that was similar. No, this had nothing to do with Julian.

Trent and I mated while under the influence of a sleeping

pill. Gabe's bright idea of drugging me so that the bond between Alex and me would be broken because he knew I would fight it. No one took into account that while Trent took my blood, he would be affected by the drug also. He had broken not only my blood bond with Alex but my mating bond, too, when our passion ignited.

Now that I thought about it, I knew Hugh better than I had known either of them—and longer. That did not settle my nerves, though, and I focused on the part of myself that knew that having Hugh at my side would make a substantial difference in what was to come. If only we had someone who could see the future. Someone who could tell us that tying myself to him was the right way to go about this.

While I did like Hugh, I wasn't in love with him. He was sexy and very handsome. His body was perfect, and his mind was sharp. Even though we hadn't spoken much about his job or life, I could tell that he was an intelligent man.

When he had first come to me, I'd had someone do an extensive background check on him. Reading it had almost put me to sleep because it was so middle-class typical and boring. A single mother raised him in a changing world. He had done well in school, played a few sports, went on to college, did four years in the Marines, joined DHS, and worked his way up.

He had never been married, and there were no children on record. I was aware of a few girlfriends, but nothing serious. His credit was above average, and his bank account, while not significant, was comfortable for a single man.

Yet, I didn't know what he liked to do on his off time or what he enjoyed eating. Again, I hadn't known that about Julian or Trent, and I had come to love them both very much. Did I love Hugh? No. Could I love Hugh? I wasn't sure, although I'd like to think I could.

I wasn't doing this for love, though. I was doing this for my breed, for my position, for the future of our lives. That was what mattered, and nothing else.

Clayton and I had had a very long conversation. He wanted to make sure I knew what I was doing. By the time we'd finished our talk, he saw my side, and while he wasn't sure it would work out, he was prepared to help me any way that he could, even by conducting the transition himself since Hugh's father wasn't an option.

As Hugh arrived at my apartment, I wavered. Did I want to do this? No, but it was my responsibility as the mistress. I had to put aside my wants and desires and do what was needed.

Hugh was nervous, and having everyone in the apartment when he arrived was probably a bad idea. It wasn't intentional. Rex was again trying to talk me out of doing it. He had been on my case since I made the announcement. Garrett, as usual, remained neutral, saying that he stood behind whatever choice I made.

After everyone left, I took Hugh's hands in mine. "Thank you, Hugh. Your life is about to become so much more. You will never know how much this means to me."

He gave me a crooked smile. "You're welcome, Kristin."

I kissed him tenderly once and then left my apartment for Clayton to take over. Ryker and Conner were there to help too, and I knew that in a few hours, life would be different for everyone.

Angelina and I went into her apartment. "You're nervous."

"A little. I keep wondering if I am doing the right thing."

"I think you are," she told me. "At least I'd like to think that you are."

"What is that supposed to mean?"

She cackled for a moment and then grew serious. "You are never one to jump on an idea that you didn't think held merit. I agree with you that this could be good for you, for all of us, but it makes me nervous too."

"What makes you most nervous?"

"The fact that you don't know him. None of us know Hugh all that well."

"I was thinking about that earlier. I didn't know Julian or Trent when I mated with them, and look at how those turned out."

"Yeah, you got yourself killed for one of them, and the other killed himself."

I glared at her. "Cut that shit out."

"Sorry, low blow. I guess I'm concerned about how this will affect you. What if it doesn't amplify your powers, but hinders them instead?"

"I don't think that will happen, not after what we saw at the club the other night. However, it is something that I have considered. Angelina, I have to ask you a favor."

"What?"

I inhaled slowly and then released it. "If, for some reason, it does not help me, I am going to need you to break our mating."

"What?" she snapped, her eyes practically bulging from their sockets.

"You heard me, and don't think I haven't noticed the way you look at him. You like him."

"Just because I like him, does not mean that I want to mate him."

"I know that, but—" I paused and lowered my voice so that I knew it was low enough that anyone outside in the hallway would not hear. "I don't trust Hugh one hundred percent, Lena. I can't have someone at my side that I can't trust, and that can't help me. I'm not asking you to remain mated with him, but to break our mating until we can find someone else for him to bond to."

"Why don't you trust him, Kris?"

"I'm not sure. Maybe Josh's worry has rubbed off on me a bit, who knows."

"Okay, but if this mating doesn't work, what are you going to do?"

"If mating with Hugh doesn't work, then I am going to mate with Clayton."

She wrinkled her nose. "You'd sleep with him?"

I laughed. "I already have, once, a long time ago. It was okay."

"Just okay? Not earth-shattering like Julian?"

"Nothing was as earth-shattering as Julian. Even Trent didn't hold a candle to the chemistry that Julian and I shared, and I loved Trent a lot."

She hesitated before she began to speak. "Kristin, I know I probably shouldn't bring this up, but have you ever considered that it might have been your blood that made Trent kill himself?"

I stared at my sister, my lips parted in surprise. After I had learned that Trent had staked himself, that very thing was all I could think about. In the few months leading up to his death, Trent had begun to act strangely. He was confused at times, easily angered, and lethargic at others.

"Are you suggesting that my blood drove him mad?"

She shrugged. "Yeah, but I asked more pleasantly."

My eyes closed tightly as I exhaled. "Yes, I had considered it."

"I figured you had. You don't think it will hurt Hugh, do you?"

"I guess only time with tell on that. But if Hugh does start to exhibit unusual behavior, we will take him out."

Her brows jumped. "You mean kill him?"

I frowned at her and lowered my voice. "Only if we have to, but we can make it look like someone else did it. I don't want to do that; trust me. I want this to work, but if something happens, I'm going to need your help with it."

"Fine," she replied. "Do you plan on mating with him tonight after he transitions?"

"I'm not sure I will have a choice. Ever since I tasted Hugh's blood, I crave it. I don't think I'll be able to hold myself back when he takes my vein today."

"Well, enjoy that," she muttered.

"Hey, I know you like Hugh, Angelina. You can pretend that you don't, and I'm sorry that I am doing this to you."

She put her hand up. "Don't. I get it. Maybe I do like the guy, but you did have him first. If he helps you, then I can handle it. I want you at your strongest so that we can get rid of Portage."

"Agreed, but if this works and strengthens me like we think it will, we will search for another reborn for you."

* * *

FIVE HOURS LATER, I was in my office reading over field reports when Clayton reached out to me. *"Transition is done. He went through it nicely. Quicker than I expected."*

"That's good. I'll be up soon."

I stared at the picture on the other side of the room and sighed. The step that I was about to take would lead me down a new path—one we didn't know much about. It was going to be a new chapter of my life. One so very different than where my life in this world had started over forty years ago.

As I reached the door, I paused. "I wish you were here, Alex. You could tell me if I was doing the right thing." My gaze drifted to his son, and then to Julian. What I wouldn't do to have any of them here with me now.

I shoved my feelings deep down and went upstairs. Clayton, Ryker, and Conner were in my living room, telling me how it went. We laughed for a few moments, and then we heard Hugh stir in my room.

Hugh was sitting up when I stepped in, and I spoke very softly. "How are you?"

His eyes were wide, the blue brighter than before, and I fought a shiver. "I can hear everything, feel everything."

"You'll learn to control it so that you aren't overwhelmed. It will take some time, Hugh, but you'll figure it out."

I stood back as the guys talked to Hugh about releasing his canines, and he figured it out quickly. He latched on to Ryker and Conner, but his eyes remained glued to mine. The bonds that Hugh was building right now were not required, but I wanted two other people to be able to protect him and watch over him when I was busy. I did not doubt that Hugh would become a target as soon as people learned of him.

I trusted Ryker and Conner, and I knew they would tell me if they felt or heard something that I should be concerned with. They were going to be my eyes and ears to him after this mating took place.

Hugh shoved Conner's wrist away, growling, "Go." They were barely out of the way when Hugh was wrapping his arms around me, his mouth already moving toward my neck.

I twisted out of his grasp and threw him backward with a strike to the chest. "Lay down, tiger. We have time. Stay."

He growled rather ferally at me but remained where he was as I undressed. His need slammed into me; his bonding scent filled the room, and his craving for blood almost took me to my knees—finally, someone who could take my vein. I almost whimpered as my need exploded through me. Not just for sex, but for his teeth to be in my neck and pulling from me.

It had been so long since I had been in this state, a state in which it was hard to think straight, and instinct screamed to take over. I forced myself to get him fully undressed, although he was fighting my compulsion to stay in place. He would probably be pissed that I had compelled him at all, but I needed to control this moment, and not let him. That lasted until I crawled on the bed, and then he shattered the compulsion, grabbed my arm, and in one swift move, had me under him.

Our eyes locked. "We have all night. Kiss me, Hugh." I felt the strength building in him, and I welcomed it. I touched his face lightly, knowing that his senses were in overdrive right now. His lips touched mine gently for only a few seconds before he took possession of them. I whimpered into his mouth as his bonding scent poured over us. He shifted his body between my legs and drove himself home in one strong surge. He moaned a few times as if he were dying, but I knew that it was from the intensity of his senses.

Hugh released my mouth, his eyes skimming over my face and latching on to my neck. My blood was pounding in my veins, screaming for him to latch on. I needed him as I had never needed anyone before, and my words came out on a plea. "Take my vein, Hugh, please—take my vein now."

He dove for my neck, snapping his powerful jaws onto it, and sinking his teeth in. His body tensed immediately, then shook, and his hips rammed forward. I felt my blood mixing with his, the power building, and he groaned. Even if I had wanted to, I couldn't have held myself back. I was almost as blood-starved as he was, and I struck his neck and pulled from his vein.

His taste was strong, heady, and it ran down my throat as his body convulsed over me. I had felt this mating bond before, knew the intensity of it, but it still shook me to the core. I forced myself to stay focused and let his memories flash through my mind. Nameless people and faces slipping through so quickly, I could barely grasp their images. A few pictures were darkened and hazy as if hidden deep down someplace, but I managed to take a mental snapshot of them. I pulled from his vein again as the two of us hit that higher pinnacle and exploded over.

I removed my teeth from his neck as I cried out. His fangs released from my soft tissue as he tried to control his ragged breathing. Whether I had wanted to mate with him or not, it was done. Now only time will tell if it was the right choice. I joked with Hugh for a moment as I worked over the images that I had gotten from him and found myself frowning slightly.

"What's wrong?" he asked me.

I told him that work needed me and that I would send someone else to feed him. His concern was almost funny about feeding on another woman and the possibility of having sex with them. Even when I told him I didn't mind, he seemed bothered by that. I guess I remembered that feeling when I was younger. When I had been mated to Alex the second time, I had slept with only him, so I understood.

I quickly went into the bathroom and cleaned up, standing in front of the mirror for a moment, wrestling with an image I had seen in his mind. I stepped out, needing to check on something that was burning inside of me as quickly as I could.

"I'll be back when I can be."

"See you then," he said, and I walked to my apartment door, then opened and closed it. I stood there and waited.

"It's done," I heard Hugh say to someone a moment later, and I closed my eyes, trying to concentrate on the voice on the other end of the phone, but I couldn't quite hear it. "Yeah, I'm in."

Hugh was quiet for a moment. "They not only turned me, but I am now mated to the mistress."

I could just make out a laugh and the loud words after that. "Mated to the mistress? Are you serious?"

"Yes," Hugh told him, and I clenched my jaw. Hugh was quiet for a moment before he spoke again, and his words were like acid in my veins. "Yes, Master, I do."

Mother—fucker! I opened the door again and slipped out without a sound. The minute I was outside, I went right to Joshua's apartment. He was standing in the kitchen, eating a hot dog.

"I want you to think of Alex's death," I snapped at him as I strode directly to him, his mouth full, his cheeks puffed up like a chipmunk. "I want you to think of his death now, Josh."

He looked shocked, and he forced the food down his throat. "Why? What's wrong, Kristin?"

"Just fucking do it!" I snapped at him, and while he seemed concerned, I felt his memories shifting. I latched on to his neck before he even knew I was going to. I had to see his vivid memories, and this was the best way.

A deep voice echoed through Josh's mind—a face appeared—a man with a blade. I jerked my teeth from his neck and licked it once before spinning and walking away.

"What the fuck was that, Kris?" he called out to me.

"Nothing, I just needed to double-check something. I'll be in my office; I do not want to be disturbed."

CHAPTER EIGHT

ANGELINA

I would do whatever I could for my sister, even mate with someone if that's what she asked me to do. Of course, the thought of being mated to Hugh wasn't a horrible one, but then again, I hadn't thought my mating to Cameron would have been bad either.

Speaking of Cameron, I wondered where he was hiding. Maybe I should locate him and work off some of the sexual tension crackling under my skin. It was too bad we were all stuck inside tonight. I could have used a few hours at the club. Hot bodies grinding on the dance floor, a random hookup, a couple of sips of young blood might be exactly what I needed.

Perhaps I needed to convince Kristin to add a dance club here in the hotel. That way, we didn't have to go out, but we could still be around people and work out our frustrations. Now that was a thought. God knew there was room here.

While this was a working hotel, it was more frequented by our breed than by humans. Humans did stay here—some out of curiosity, some looking for a life change. Adding a club to the lounge would add profit to the hotel, although it wasn't like we needed the money. After being alive for so many years, we had all acquired wealth. Plus, Kristin had inherited not only Trent's money, but Alex's too. The woman was set for life.

While Kristin was aware of what was happening around the hotel, I was more involved in it than she was. I hadn't planned to be involved, but she was busy with breed business, and I'd slowly taken over. In the beginning, I used to ask her if I could change things; she always told me to do what I wanted or thought would work. Eventually, I stopped asking and just went with my ideas. The hotel had prospered, and as I thought of the dance club, I knew it would bring in more money. Between entry and liquor, it could be a gold mine. Huh—who knew I would have a knack for the hospitality industry.

I made my way down to the main floor and walked around, checking out the main floor and letting my mind dwell on the possibility. After that, I spent a few hours in the lounge, relaxing with everyone else who could feel the tension in the building. I also helped at the front desk for a few minutes so Vivian could take a dinner break and was stepping off the elevator on my floor when Josh stepped out of his apartment.

"What the fuck is up with Kris?" he asked.

I froze midstep and eyed him carefully. "As far as I know, she's still getting it on with her mate, why?"

He shook his head. "No, she's not. She was in here about forty-five minutes ago, demanded that I think of Alex's death, and then she bit me before she stalked out, snapping at me that she wasn't to be disturbed in her office."

I stared at her apartment door, then glanced toward the elevator. Had the mating not happened? I turned back to her door. "Has anyone checked on Hugh?"

"I haven't. I don't give a shit how the fuck he is. He could be dead for all I care," he growled as he hit the button for the elevator.

I had him against the wall a moment after his finger came off the button, my forearm at his throat, my fangs down as I hissed, "Don't be an ass, Josh. We need him, or more importantly, Kristin needs him. The last thing you want is Kristin to lose this right now, and you better change your fucking attitude before she comes down on you. You are already walking a thin line with her. You keep pushing, and she's going to find someone else to stand at her side. Do you want that?"

I knew he didn't, and the look in his eyes said the same. I released his neck and stepped back. "I'll go check on Hugh before I find my sister."

"Whatever floats your boat, Lena," he said dryly as the elevator door opened, and he flashed around me and into the metal box.

I stood by her apartment door and listened for a moment but didn't hear anything. I stepped in slowly, still not hearing anything, and sniffed the air. I could smell blood, but it wasn't overbearing. The most potent scent in the apartment was Hugh's bonding scent, and I shivered. I went toward the bedroom. The bed was a mess, but Hugh wasn't among it. "Hugh?"

I took a moment to focus on him since I'd had a brief taste of his blood, and I found him, but not in the apartment. I hit the stairs that led to the roof and stepped out into the night air to see him standing at the edge, staring over the city. He glanced back at me, his eyes slipping down my body and then back up before he smiled.

"I didn't know this existed. It's pretty nice up here."

I began to approach, making sure to keep my cool and pretend I hadn't just seen him checking me out. "It is nice. This is her private sanctuary. Kristin likes to come up here and think. Where is she, by the way?"

"She said she had work that needed her attention. I was

wandering around her apartment and found the door for up here. She won't mind, will she?"

I stopped next to him, sniffing the air lightly. They had mated. I wondered what pulled Kris away from his side. Usually, newly mated couples didn't want to leave each other until they had to.

I shook my head. "No, she won't. How are you doing?"

He grinned, his blue eyes sparkling brightly. "I'm kind of flying on a high right now. Everything is so much more—just more."

I laughed. "Yes, it is. Everything went alright?"

He turned to study me, and I shifted my gaze over his handsome features. "Are you asking if Kristin and I mated? If you are, the answer is yes." My fingers itched to drift over his graying temples, but I resisted.

I chuckled. "I could already tell that."

"You can?"

I stood beside him, my forearms resting on the railing, and looked out over the city. "Yes, your scent has changed. It was very smoky before, and now it is a bit sweeter, still smoky, though."

He leaned toward me, inhaling deeply, and I turned to see what he was doing, our faces only a couple of inches apart. I cocked a brow. "May I help you?"

He laughed. "No, I just wanted to know what you smelled like."

"And?"

"And I happen to like peaches." He hadn't moved back, and my gaze slipped to his lips momentarily. "Although you smell slightly sweeter than just peaches."

"Cream?" I suggested softly as I continued to stare at him.

The left side of his mouth lifted slightly. "Yes, peaches and cream. I bet that would be an enjoyable flavor to have running down my throat."

I stepped back, laughing as I slammed a lid on my sexual urges. Holy shit, if Kris weren't my sister, I'd have that man under me, and I'd be at his throat in a heartbeat. "You just mated with my sister, and here you are hitting on me for my blood."

He chuckled. "My bad. Sorry, I guess my hormones are a little all over the place," he paused. "And you are a stunning woman, Angelina."

"Lena, my friends call me Lena." I kept my focus on the city and not him. I didn't need him knowing that his words affected me.

"Is that what I am? A friend?" His voice was husky as he spoke.

"Well, unless you'd rather consider yourself my brother-in-law"—I turned to nail him with a hard look—"and in that case, it's not okay to be letting your hormones run rampant around me."

"But it's okay if we are just friends?" His brow lined.

I pursed my lips. "Actually, it's not. I've tasted your blood, Hugh. I know how incredible and intense it is. Kristin said she has been craving it since she first tasted it. I have to admit, I have too, so it's better if we keep the distance between us."

He shifted toward me. "You know Kristin mentioned that she doesn't mind if I'm with other people."

"No, she wouldn't mind if those other people were nobodies. I would be a different story." I didn't tell him that was because I'd take him for myself and end up breaking their mating.

He sighed as he turned away and looked over the city. "You're right. I'm sorry. My head is all over the place tonight."

"It's okay. You get a pass right now, but next time, we might have a problem."

"Alright, next time you can kick my ass." He grinned at me and winked.

I tossed my head back and laughed. "You do not want me to kick your ass."

He eyed me sideways and shrugged. "Might be interesting."

I decided it was better to let that comment go. "You said Kristin had work to do?"

"Yeah, right after we finished, she took off."

"Did she seem okay?"

"Yeah, she seemed fine. She even sent two women up to feed me, but I told them I was fine."

"You turned down more blood?" I stared at him, slightly shocked.

"Yeah, I wasn't interested."

"Okay, well, I better go check in with the boss and make sure she doesn't need any help with whatever she is working on."

"Hey, Angelina." I turned back to him. "Um, I wasn't interested in more blood, but where should I go for food? I'm starving."

"You can go down to the restaurant. It's open twenty-four seven. Eventually, you won't need to eat as often, especially after regular feedings on Kristin, but for now, you'll need both. Kristin doesn't keep much in her fridge except junk food."

"Somehow, I didn't expect that." He chuckled.

"Prepare yourself; there is a lot that you probably didn't expect when it comes to my sister."

"I'll take your word for it. Mind if I ride down with you?"

"Suit yourself," I told him over my shoulder. He followed me down to the apartment and toward the elevator.

"So who lives up here?"

"Kristin and I have the largest apartments on the floor. Josh is next to her, Rex and Clayton are on the opposite side, and Lorna, Clayton's granddaughter, has the other one on our floor. Most of the other sentinels and family are on the two floors below, eight and nine. Below them is our main office floor, and then the sixth floor is more office space. The other four floors have hotel rooms."

"Do people come here to stay?"

"Yep, a lot of our breed stays here while traveling, and we do have humans that stay here too." We were in the elevator, and it stopped at the eighth floor. "Before you go down to eat, you should probably learn where her office is."

He followed me off the elevator, and I paused when I saw the group of people standing near one of the office doors. They glanced back at us. "What's going on?"

Lainey shook her head. "Nothing, at least I don't think it's anything."

I frowned at her. *"What's going on, Lainey?"*

"Do you know what's wrong with Kristin?"

"No, is something wrong with her?"

"Um, you might want to check on her yourself." I nodded and then turned to Hugh. "Hugh, this is Lainey, she's Kristin's assistant and Lorna's daughter. This is Abina, my daughter, and Beatrix, Alex's daughter. I think you know Paxton already from the club."

He smiled at each of them, but seemed perplexed. "It's nice to meet you all."

As we walked away, he said softly. "It's odd to think that those ladies are daughters when they all look the same age as their parents; Lainey looks younger, though."

"Lainey is younger; she's only twenty, hasn't transitioned yet. Abina is about to transition here soon; she's thirty-four."

"I didn't realize you had a daughter. Who is the father?"

"Cameron."

"Were you two together long?"

"Not for long, a few years, but that was a long time ago."

"Were you two mated?

"Yes."

"Have you ever been mated to anyone else?" he asked.

"Nope. I prefer to be on my own." I didn't bother to tell him that one day he might be tied to me. Better not to let that out, lest he have any ideas.

I knocked on her door and then pushed it open without waiting for a reply. I was pretty sure she would know that we were here. No doubt, her blood was reacting to Hugh being near.

She sat behind her desk, her feet kicked up on the desktop, reading something on a tablet as if she didn't have a care in the world. She lifted her head slowly, glanced past me, and then let loose a very practiced smile. "Hi, what brings you guys down here?"

"I heard you were working, so I checked in on Hugh, and he said he was hungry. I thought I'd show him where you work; that way, he will know where to find you in the future."

I had expected her to get up, maybe come over to greet him, but she remained right where she was. I shifted so I could face Hugh. "So this is where she works. Exciting, isn't it?"

He chuckled, stepped further into the room, and glanced around. His gaze paused on the picture beside the door, and he gravitated toward it. "Who are all these people?"

I shot Kristin a look; she nodded slightly. "That was taken about forty years ago, our close friends and family. That's when Alex was mated to Courtney, and she's holding Beatrix whom you just met. Kristin and Trent were together then, and that's little Rex. He was so sweet back then." Kristin chuckled from her desk. "That is Julian and Lyssa. Lyssa was Lorna's mother."

I paused as I stared at the picture. "Some of the other people were human; they are gone now, of course, except Mick. Mick was turned; you'll see him around here once in a while. He used to be Kristin's partner back when she was a cop."

Hugh's face had snapped toward Kristin. "I thought turning humans was illegal?"

"It is," Kristin stated casually—almost too plainly. What was going on? "Back then, it wasn't, and it was new. We didn't know too much about it. We have learned a lot since."

"Why is it that humans can't be turned now?"

Kristin and I shared a glance, and she sighed. "Human-turned are unpredictable. Women, especially. There is a whole process that they need to go through after they are turned, and we can't always guarantee the outcome. We've had to put down a lot of the human-turned because they become too violent."

Hugh leaned closer to the picture and pointed at someone. "Who is that? He looks familiar."

I glanced at the person he was pointing to. "That is Gabriel."

"Is he still alive?"

"As far as we know." I glanced back at my sister; her brow hiked on one side. "You said he looked familiar; when did you see him?" I asked.

Hugh looked thoughtful for a moment. "I don't know exactly when, but I'm pretty sure I did speak with him. I think it was down south a few months ago. Might have been in North or South Carolina, could have been Georgia."

I pointed at Olivia in the picture. "Was she with him?"

He shook his head. "He wasn't with any women, a couple of men, but none of them would give me their names."

Kristin and I shared another glance, and I wondered if Olivia was still alive. I would have thought that if she were dead, I would have known since I had sired her, but then again, maybe I wouldn't have.

"Are you all not in contact anymore?" Hugh asked as he looked between us.

"No," Kristin said softly. "Olivia was one of those human-turned that was a mistake. Even though she retained her humanity to a degree, she became increasingly violent. I made them leave before I had to put her down."

"Put her down? You say that like she was a dog," Hugh stated with a frown. "I thought she was your friend."

"She was my best friend, Hugh, but that was a different life-time ago. I can't have one set of standards for our breed and one for my personal friends. That is not how it works when you are in a place of power. Perhaps if she had tried to control herself and didn't brag about all the kills that she did, I might have been able to protect her."

He glanced back at the picture and nodded as if he understood.

"What are you working on?" I asked Kristin to change the subject as Hugh started to walk around the office and check things out.

"Just work," she said aloud, then directed her next comment to me. *"Can you please get him out of my office?"*

"Why can't he be in your office?"

"I don't want him in here, or on this floor right now. Not until we know more about him."

"Is something going on?"

"No, I just have a lot on my mind."

"Alright, well, we'll let you get back to work, and I'll make sure your man gets something to eat."

Hugh hesitated as if he weren't sure if he should approach her or not. His blood was probably telling him one thing, while her demeanor said something else. He ended up smiling at her and then stepped back toward me. "You want to join us?"

"Thanks, but I have a lot to get done. Enjoy yourself," she said, and I spiked a brow her way as I turned.

"What is going on?"

"Nothing, I'll talk to you later," she muttered as I stepped out.

I took Hugh's arm and led him back toward the elevator. "What was down that other hallway?"

"Ah, boring offices and conference rooms—nothing exciting. Let's find some food. I'm in the mood for a big steak and a strong drink."

As I punched the button for the bottom floor, I wondered

what Kristin knew that she wasn't saying. She wasn't herself, and she definitely was not acting like a newly mated woman who couldn't keep her hands off her man. I eyed him cautiously; had she already realized that it been a mistake to mate with him?

CHAPTER NINE

HUGH

After Kristin left, I took a shower, and when I finished, I wasn't quite sure what to do with myself. I began to wander around her apartment, stopping to look over each photograph again and the small array of knickknacks she had scattered around her living room. Random figurines and odd pieces of glass that probably held stories that maybe one day I would hear.

In her kitchen, I pulled open the fridge and chuckled. There was a variety of soda and junk food, along with a compartment that held bags of blood. My fingertips tingled, and my new teeth began to vibrate in my gums. I slammed the door and rushed out of the kitchen.

Yeah, I might have consumed blood a few times already, but that didn't mean that this whole thing didn't freak me the fuck out now that I was alone and didn't have anything to distract me.

There was a knock at the door, and I opened it to find two females standing there. "Hi, I'm not sure if you remember me, but I'm Cora, and this is Lydia. Kristin sent us up to feed you."

While they were both attractive women, and the urge to feed

was building in me, I just didn't feel right about it. "I appreciate that, ladies, but I'm doing pretty good."

They glanced at one another. "Are you sure? The mistress thought you might need more blood after your transition."

"I am sure, but thank you. I feel pretty good, but if something changes, I'll make sure to find you two again. Thank you."

Lydia spoke up. "If you are concerned about having sex with us, we can make sure you just feed."

I laughed slightly. "I really am okay, but thank you."

They said goodbye, and I could tell they weren't sure what to think of being turned down. I closed the door and glanced around before I walked to the other side of the room. I stood at the window, staring out into the darkened city as I thought about what had happened already tonight.

The process hadn't been horrible. Yeah, it had hurt like a bitch, but the memory of that was already fading. The change hadn't been as shocking or traumatic as I had anticipated. No, the biggest shock had been waking up and seeing everything so clearly, hearing things that I never thought possible, and the intense, overwhelming, obsessive need to be with Kristin the moment I saw her.

A shiver zipped down my spine. Fuck! In an instant, I was hard again, my fancy new teeth throbbing in my jaw like my dick was in my pants. I needed to do something, anything to get my mind off it! I turned away from the window and began to wander around her place again. I opened all the doors, peered into a few closets, and then found a stairway that went up. She was on the top floor, so that could only lead to the roof.

I took the stairs and pushed open the heavy outer door. There was a garden balcony, and I grinned as I glanced around. Thank god! Fresh fucking air. Was this her private sanctuary? There were a couple of chaise lounges, a large table and six chairs, tiny sparkling lights around the seating area, and plants, lots of plants for this early in the year; maybe they were fake. I passed them, not really caring, and headed toward the railing.

My gaze skimmed over the city in front of me, and I took notice of details that I'd never noticed before. I could see things, vibrant colors even in the darkness, that generally wouldn't have been noticeable, and the sounds were incredible. Someplace down below a dog barked, and someone dropped something into a dumpster, a person sneezed, another laughed nervously. Transports moved along the streets below, and while they usually would have seemed silent, I could hear the whisper of the engines up here.

I don't know how long I stood there, taking it all in and wondering what was next in my life when I heard the metal scrape of the door behind me opening. Hopefully that was Kristin coming back; sadly, as I looked over my shoulder, I saw it wasn't.

Angelina joined me, and I tried to keep myself in check, but it was hard. My mind and body were all over the place, and after pulling her scent deep into my lungs, I wanted more. Damn, I wish Kristin was done with her work. I could imagine taking her up here from behind, my dick deep inside of her, while I sucked from her neck. My body was ready to explode all over again.

Luckily, my stomach growled and reminded me of my other hunger, and I followed Lena down to the elevator. I was slightly surprised when she offered to show me where Kristin worked. Probably useful information to know now that we were together. The ladies that I'd been introduced to were nice and studied me carefully, but I wasn't able to read them very well. I wondered briefly what they thought of all of this, or if they even had an opinion.

Inside Kristin's office, I was disappointed that she didn't get out of her seat and come to me. The minute I saw her, I wanted to bend her over her desk. I wanted to lose myself in her and enjoy the taste of her blood as it filled my mouth, but she didn't seem to feel the same. Was that normal? Maybe how I felt wasn't normal.

Or was it because of who she was, or who I was? Maybe mating with her hadn't been a good idea, but then again, something inside of me said it was exactly what I needed to do. Perhaps my need to have her again so soon was merely my body still adjusting to the transition. It had to be normal. Maybe it was normal? Who the fuck knew!

Kristin and her sister shared a long look, and then Kristin chuckled to herself and winked at me. Okay, a wink was good, right? I had no clue where we stood with one another.

We left her in her office to work, and Angelina and I took the elevator down to the bottom floor. "You can get food in the bar or the restaurant. I'm going to choose the bar tonight because I think we both can use a couple of drinks," she told me as we walked along.

When we entered the crowded lounge, the volume went from fifty to zero in a second. Almost every conversation stopped, and necks craned to look our way.

"Um, why are they all staring at me, Angelina?"

She laughed. "Because you are big news, Hugh." She slapped me on the back and headed to the bar as the conversation in the room started up again. The sound was almost overwhelming as people leaned forward and talked over one another. I wanted to stick my fingers in my ears and run from the room. How did they deal with this noise?

Lena turned to me at the bar and leaned forward, speaking softly. "You have to turn it down mentally. It's like your brain has a volume control now, and you need to adjust it as needed."

"Yeah, well, how the fuck do you do that?"

"Just tell yourself to lower the volume."

My gaze bounced to her sexy lips momentarily. "That easy, huh?"

"Yeah, that easy."

How fucking wrong was it for me to want to pull her into my lap? She hiked a brow and pulled herself back, laughing. "You need to protect your thoughts, Hugh, and yes, it would be wrong to pull me into your lap."

"Wait? Why? Did you hear that?" I glanced around me and found a few people smirking my way.

She laughed. "I'm pretty sure the entire bar heard that if they were listening."

People were still staring at me, and a few laughed. A couple of women gave me come-hither looks. My gaze passed over Josh and bounced back. He stood in the corner with Rex, neither of them laughing. They stared at me with open hostility.

"They don't like me very much, do they?" I asked as I turned back to Angelina.

"Don't mind them. Josh and Rex are both overprotective, and one is just jealous because he can't have her." She spoke loudly. I did not doubt that they both heard what she said, but she didn't seem to care.

I watched her for a moment. "You and Kristin could hear my thoughts earlier in her office, couldn't you?"

Angelina snickered. "Oh, yes, but you are not the first man to want to put her over a desk."

"Is that why she winked at me?"

"She found your mental musings humorous," she replied, but for just a moment, she looked concerned about something.

Well, shit. I needed to figure things out quickly here. "Someone was teaching me how to protect my thoughts, and I thought I was doing pretty good, but now I wonder if I was doing anything."

"Someone was helping you? Who?"

"A woman that I know, her name is Bridgette." I turned the glass around in front of me that had been delivered. "When I first started working for the task force, she gave me some information to help me."

Angelina's voice dropped. "She gave you information about us? Like what?"

"Relax, Angelina, nothing important, trust me. She told me general things like eating habits and family dynamics. She would not talk about anything important."

"Who did you say this person was?"

"I said her name was Bridgette."

"How did you get her to talk?"

I sipped my drink and couldn't hold back the image of having sex with her on the counter. "I had my ways."

Angelina shocked the hell out of me as she threw her head back and belted out a laugh. I would have cringed from the decibel level, but my eyes locked on to the vein in her neck as her long hair fell back, and it took everything in me not to move off my stool.

Angelina was still laughing as she turned to me, seemingly oblivious to my lusty need to take her vein. "She compelled you to have sex with her," she said around a laugh. "Bridgette does that all the time."

"You know her?"

She kept snickering as she sipped her drink. "Yes, she used to be a good friend of mine. She was forever enticing men to sleep with her. She would compel them. She used to compel her husband to watch, but I think he got so into it that she doesn't have to compel him anymore."

My jaw hung down, and she pushed it closed. "Did you think you were special, Hugh? Don't take offense to it; she's a nympho. I'm sure she didn't tell you anything important. She doesn't know anything important. She is a bit of an airhead."

"She didn't come across that way to me."

"Yeah, well, your mind was a little twisted in her presence." She stared at me hard. "How many times were you with her?"

"Three."

Angelina shook her head and laughed again as I busied myself looking anywhere but at her.

"How do I protect my thoughts?" I asked her when she calmed down.

"You figured out how to turn the sound down, right?"

I nodded. While it was still loud in here, it was manageable now. "Yes."

"Build a wall in your mind and keep it up. We all have different types of walls. Sometimes we block everything; other times, just our dark and twisted thoughts; sometimes we are only blocked to certain people. You might want to block your lustful thoughts for others for a while until you get used to the feelings."

I stared at her. "Does this constant need to have sex ever go away?"

Her eyes sparkled mischievously. "No. We just get better at hiding our desires or finding people to sate them on."

Ugh! I was pretty sure that right then, I would have been willing to sate them on anyone. I glanced toward the door; Rex and Josh were still glaring at me. Okay, so not anyone.

"So, I just build a wall, like a brick wall? What kind of wall?"

"Any type that you want to build. Whatever kind you think will block out the noise or the nosy people who want to invade your mind."

"And then no one can hear what you don't want them to?"

"Mostly."

I frowned at her. "What do you mean, mostly?"

"There are a few of our kind that can read your thoughts no matter what you do to hide them. Cameron is like that. He can see right through your walls."

I laughed. "I bet that comes in handy."

"It does unless you're mated to him." She smirked, and we

shared a laugh and ordered our food as the bartender appeared in front of us.

After we did, I sat back and tried to relax. "Does Kris always work this hard?"

Angelina laughed. "Oh, yes. Sorry, you just mated a workaholic. My sister is very intense, and she works her ass off. She has a lot to oversee and spends much of her day communicating with other masters around the world to make sure things are running smoothly while still making sure that our breed and humans here in the U.S. are safe."

"What do you do?"

"Me? I look pretty and entertain everyone." She smiled sweetly, and I laughed at her. "Fine, most of the time, I'm on the road. I delve into sensitive things for her or help teams that are investigating certain things."

"Investigating? What do you mean by that?"

She lifted a brow. "You were a cop, don't you know what investigation means?"

"Of course, I know what it means for a cop, but I'm talking about what you do. Is it the same?"

She nodded and continued. "Yes, we do the same thing. We collect evidence, speak to witnesses or victims, and determine if a member of the breed did something wrong."

"And if they are found guilty, what happens?"

She shrugged. "Depends on what kind of stupid shit they did and how many people it has affected. Sometimes a severe warning is left, and that is enough. Other times, it takes a harsher approach."

"You mean killing them, right?"

"Yes."

"How many have you killed?"

One of her brows hiked high. "Vampires or humans?"

I opened my mouth to say vampires, but closed it as I frowned. "Wait, you have killed both humans *and* vampires?"

She sighed. "First of all, Hugh, you have to forget that you are no longer human; you no longer belong to that world, and the rules of that race no longer apply to you."

"That's bullshit, Angelina. Answer my original questions. Have you killed humans?"

"That wasn't your original question, Hugh." She glared at me and then sighed.

"It's the question now," I grunted.

"Take a look around the room." She paused and lifted her hand, flicking it around the room. I glanced around. "How many of the people in here do you think have killed a human?"

"I don't know."

"I would be willing to bet that every single vampire in this room has killed at least one, some of them many, many more."

"And you think that's alright?"

She laughed, and her eyes skittered around the tables slightly. *"Hugh, you might want to watch your demeanor right now. You might be mated to the mistress, but you don't want to get on the wrong side of your breed."*

I pursed my lips. *"Fine."*

"Back before I knew I had a sister, when I lived with my father, Burke, I was involved in a lot of dark stuff that I am not proud of now. I killed a lot of humans and vampires."

"How long ago was that?"

"Over forty years ago. Why? Are you going to arrest me for murder, or does murder have a statute of limitations now?"

"No, I'm not going to arrest you, Angelina. I will assume that the people that you killed deserved to die."

She laughed rather jovially. "Ah, well, not all of them."

I stared at her profile. Her light-blue eyes flitted toward me and then away as I asked, "What do you mean, not all of them?"

She glanced around the room again and sighed, crossing her arms on the bar. "When my father was alive, we started testing the whole human-turned thing."

"Testing it? What the hell does that mean?"

"Trying to see how we could do it. There was an old wives' tale handed down through the generations that a human-turned could be special, so we tried to figure out how to do that."

"What exactly do you mean by special?"

She chuckled as she cocked her head. "We might be able to change your blood, but we can't take the cop out of you, can we?"

I grinned. "No."

She sighed dramatically. "Human-turned can control things, like air, water, and earth."

"They can control elements? What about fire?"

"Yes, they can, and to my knowledge, there has only ever been one who could control fire, which is good since it could kill us."

"What did you learn when you did that testing?"

She inhaled slowly, held it for a long moment, and then released it in a rush. "We learned that seventy-five percent of the women who were turned possessed elemental powers."

"What about the other twenty-five percent?"

"They never made it through the transition."

"Did these people volunteer for this?"

She shook her head. "Nope."

I stared at her. "Then where did these test subjects come from?"

"They were random people, some kidnapped, some drug addicts."

My jaw dropped just as our food arrived, but I couldn't care less about the food. I was in shock at Angelina's flippant admission.

She rolled her eyes when she peered my way. "Come on, Hugh. We live in a different world, and we live by different rules. You are going to have to get used to that. While in the past, you investigated people to make an arrest, now we investigate to kill."

"How do you get away with that?"

She picked up her fork and knife and began to cut her steak. "We don't get away with it, Hugh. Our breed knows the laws. They know what is expected of them. If they break the law, they are punished. It's as simple as that. Humans should use us as examples. We have a lot less criminal activity than they do."

"Yeah, I don't see that happening anytime soon." I cut into my steak and savored the first bite.

"So has your opinion changed of me now that you know I am a serial killer?"

I laughed. "A serial killer, huh?"

She shrugged. "Seems like the most appropriate description."

"How many people do you think you have killed in your life?"

Her light-blue eyes held mine for a moment. "I don't think you want to know that answer, Hugh."

"I wouldn't have asked if I didn't want to know the answer. So, what? Twenty, thirty?"

Her brow furrowed as she stared at her plate. "I have been living in this world for about forty-five years, Hugh. Before that, I was raised by a very vicious predator and trained to control or kill." She lifted her eyes to mine, and I noticed that the color had turned lighter than usual. I hadn't realized that her eyes shifted too, but it wasn't the color that captured my attention; it was the haunted look inside of them. "I've probably taken four to five hundred lives in that time, human and vampire."

I froze mid-chew, unable to make my mouth work. Did Angelina just say that she had killed nearly five hundred people? Was she fucking serious? I tried to swallow and choked slightly. A hard slap landed on my back, and I practically jumped out of my chair as I turned to see Ryker grinning down at me.

"Don't go choking on your food after all that work that we

did today. I'd hate to lose you so soon." Ryker pulled another bar stool up and grinned at Angelina. The haunted expression that had been on her features just a moment ago vanished. Back in its place was the sexy woman who seemed not to have a care in the world, but I was starting to see behind that façade. She might be a beautiful and sexy woman, but she was deadly as sin.

CHAPTER TEN

ZANDER

*I*t had been a few weeks since Laura had made the thoughts vanish from my mind, and during that time —when she wasn't around—I tried to figure out the number of times that she might have done that to me. I could think of at least eight where I knew I had been thinking of something and —bam!—it was gone. Was she the reason? Could she be the reason that I couldn't see the mental memories or dreams more clearly? Had she fucked with my mind so many times that my thoughts, or fantasies, or whatever the fuck they were could no longer be seen or heard clearly?

I stared at the rushing waves in front of me as I sat on the hard-packed sand. My thoughts were as turbulent as the ocean water, rolling forward and then sucking back, only to come crashing forward again. Sometimes both the water and my visions came closer, but then both would get pulled away again before they even got within reach.

Glimpses of things churned in my skull—sometimes a room, a hand, a foot would flash through my mind. Other times I would move about, and a simple scent would trigger something deep within me. Pine, spices, leather, chocolate, peaches, butter, and sometimes even sugar would stop me in my tracks. Make me pause and wonder what it was about the smell that captured my attention in the first place. Were they merely fragrances that I enjoyed, or did those particular scents connect me with something else—something from my past?

I had a hard time believing that it was my past since I could remember my life, well as far back as a child could remember things. But could my past be some elaborately concocted story that my father had slipped into my mind to make me think it was real? I knew that he had done some pretty sinister shit to others; why wouldn't he do it to me?

Because I was his son, that's why.

I stared down the darkened beach and saw a couple walking hand in hand a distance away, and I sighed and glanced back at my condo. It was dark inside, but I had expected it to be. Laura was once again out hanging with friends or doing whatever she usually did while I sat around here doing nothing. No, that wasn't right. I was doing something—I was driving myself psychotic with trying to figure out how she had taken my thoughts away. When I wasn't dwelling on that, I was attempting to figure out what she had removed already.

Since that night, I'd kept my distance from her. She had to know that I was aware of what she had done, but Laura hadn't said anything, and she hadn't acted any differently, either. Was she doing it for her own good, mine, or at my father's bidding?

My phone rang through my watch, and I glanced at the face of my watch to see it was my father. Wasn't that just perfect timing? I pushed the button on the side to answer. "Yeah?"

"Zander?"

"Yes?"

"Where are you? There is a lot of noise."

"I'm sitting on the beach. What do you want?"

84

"Oh. I called to let you know that the next step in the plan is in place."

I rolled my eyes. Why did I care? He wasn't going to tell me what that plan was, so what the fuck good did it do me?

"That's great," I replied drolly as I glared at a vicious wave that slammed into the shore.

He laughed. "Don't sound so excited."

"Yeah, well, I'm not. I'll get excited when you tell me what I'm supposed to be doing and when I can get out of here and be useful."

"Don't you want to know what's going on now?"

I frowned at the speaker on my watch. "Like you're going to tell me."

He chuckled huskily. "Actually, this I do want to share with you. I know that I have been telling you repeatedly that you have to wait for things to be in place. Trust me, I've been waiting for many years for this kind of an opportunity, and I finally have it, *we* finally have it."

"What opportunity is that?"

"A way to crush the mistress."

I shook my head. "I already know that is your plan. What has happened recently that has you all excited that you might finally be putting this crazy-ass plan of yours into action?"

"I finally have an in with her."

I stared skeptically at my watch. "An in, as in someone close to the mistress?"

"Yes, my dear boy, I have someone very deep inside her organization now. He's not the only one though; I do have others there too, but this one is going to be the icing on the cake."

"Why is he so special?"

"Because he is the newest member of her family. I have it on good authority that the mistress took a new mate."

I blinked and blinked again. "The mistress is mated? When the hell did that happen?"

"Earlier tonight," he replied, sounding very proud of himself.

"Wait, you made this happen? How did you make that happen?" I was genuinely interested in hearing what he had to say about this.

"I met with him a few weeks ago after I'd heard that he was looking for me and compelled him to get close to her. I had a feeling that she would like him, and it turned out better than I had hoped."

"What had you hoped for?"

"My initial intent was just for him to get his feet in the door and be around her, make friends with her, maybe be her lover, but it turned out better than I could have hoped for, as now he is her mate."

I nodded to the empty beach. "Well, that's good to hear that you have your in."

"It is good. Now, Zander, I want you to know that since we have an in, and I'll be able to use Hugh to help us, it will only be a matter of time before I will need you to get involved."

"When?"

"Soon."

I sighed. "Same shit, different day."

"Yeah, well, this day is different. It won't be long now, Zander, and then I will tell you everything."

"I've been hearing that same bullshit for two years now, ever since I transitioned."

"This is not a plan that can be rushed, Zander. You might have been waiting for two years, but I have been waiting for a hell of a lot longer for my rightful place."

He didn't say anything further, not even goodbye, before he disconnected and hung up. I lay back in the sand, staring at the dark sky, the stars blinking at me, and my mind began to shift as words spoken from a female floated softly into my mind. *"The sky right now is like your eyes. The deep dark sapphire of night glistening with stars."*

I froze, afraid that if I blinked, the words would disappear from my mind. They didn't, though. For once, the words remained, drifting from one side of my mind to the other as they echoed. Suddenly, more words joined them. *"The depths of your eyes are like looking into the galaxy."*

I stared at the dark, inky sky above and realized that the outer ring of my eyes was very dark, just like the nighttime sky. Had someone said that to me? Or was I making more out of this little memory recall—or premonition?

I clamped my eyes closed, wishing that I knew for sure if it were past or future that this all came from. Maybe if I knew that, I would be able to deal with it better, figure out what it all meant.

I opened my eyes again and stared at the stars above. I needed to stop thinking about this. I had to put those thoughts into someplace private and hide them from Laura. I didn't want her to take them away, not before I understood them.

Instead, my mind drifted to thoughts of the mistress. Who was the man that she had mated? My father had mentioned someone named Hugh. I glanced at my watch, noting the time; would there be anything on the internet about the mistress getting mated? Maybe I could check out the guy she hooked up with and see what I could learn about him.

If he was my father's in, then perhaps that was how he was going to need my help. It might be an excellent place to start working on something. With that, I got to my feet and took one more look out over the water.

The water changed in my vision, and I was once again looking at an odd body of water, one that I had seen before. The voice from earlier was back; it was soft, but I could just make out the words, *"I know, no matter what, we will always share a part of each other. I love you, Julian, please don't ever forget that."*

As those words slipped through my mind, my heart began to ache. I put a hand to my chest, and as I blinked the vision was gone. Why did my chest hurt? Was it because of what she had said to this man—to me? No, it couldn't be me. She had called him Julian. Who the hell was Julian?

CHAPTER ELEVEN

KRISTIN

J was staring at the wall in my office, my mind spinning at an alarming rate. That son of a bitch!

Earlier tonight, I'd been nervous, but excited too. Yes, Hugh and I didn't know each other very well, but that was okay. I had decided as I stepped into my apartment after Hugh's transition that we would have plenty of time to get to know each other, and I would probably learn to love him just like I had Trent and Julian.

I knew what I would find when I joined the men and what would ultimately happen, and my body burned intensely at the possibilities. The lust that blasted out of Hugh was strong enough that any female on the floor would have felt it. I had never felt something so intense before, and it made me wonder what else would be different about him.

It took everything in me to keep it slow when he would have tried to devour my body and soul as quickly as he could. It didn't make it any easier to slow it down when I wanted him almost as much. Right then, it wasn't what Hugh could do for me as a woman. No, this intense need was about what he could give me as the mistress—and maybe because I was finally going to have someone that I could share my blood with. That single thought made my knees weak.

It was as our bodies joined, and our blood mixed that I forced myself not to flow away with the feelings. I fought to hold on and focus on the things that Hugh's mind was sharing with me. The images were mostly hazy as if blocked, but I knew what to look for. I locked on to those pictures and absorbed them.

Hugh had no clue what was happening, and he was too far into blood lust to key in on the fact that our minds were sharing things that might have been important. It was a good thing that he was otherwise distracted. Sometimes knowledge shared wasn't meant to be. With a block in his mind, I knew that I would have to be very careful with sharing anything with him.

Did that son of a bitch think that he could get one over on me?

I thought back for a second to when I had demanded Joshua think of Alex's death. As I drew his life force from his body, I confirmed that the shadowed image in Hugh's mind had been the same man who had killed Alex. How instrumental was Portage in my meeting Hugh? From what I had heard, very.

How deeply was Hugh into Joe's world? Was he merely a pawn, or was he deeply embedded in his world? Had this all been a lie from the start? Had Hugh known what he was all this time? Had he been trying to get close to me quickly so that we'd turn him before he died as a human? Is that why Hugh had wanted me to take his blood before so that I would know what he was? Had Portage known what he was?

Portage had to know. But how?

How had Portage hidden all of this from me? Hugh had mentally been a wide-open book. Yeah, I had tried to keep out of his head, but when the man thought, he thought loudly. At no time did I ever hear or feel that he was up to no good. His friendship and romantic advances had seemed genuine. Was he even aware of his connection with Portage? Had someone compelled him? Could Joe Portage compel?

I thought back to the night at the club. It had been evident that Adam and his gang were shielded, but I knew they had also been compelled—I could feel it. My biggest question was, who was strong enough to compel all of them? Were they done individually? Unless someone else had the same ability that I did, they would have had to have been. Was Joe keeping his men under lock and key, brainwashed? Is that how he was growing his army of rebels? Did Portage have any abilities himself, or did he enlist the help of others? I could control a group of people, but I usually needed assistance to make it strong enough. Could he or someone he knows do it more efficiently?

I froze, my heart stuttering slightly; was Portage a reborn? Was it possible that he was and he had been hiding that for so long?

Son of a bitch! If Portage was a reborn, he was probably one of the first on record, and he had several years on me. I would be no match for his strength—unless I were mated to a reborn— which I now was.

But if being mated to a reborn increased my strength, why would Portage want that? What was that son of a bitch up to? Did he want someone on the inside who could pass along first-hand knowledge of what we were doing?

That had to be the answer. That sneaky son of a bitch. I glared out the window into the city, wondering how Portage knew that Hugh was a reborn. How long had Portage been working this plan? What exactly had Hugh been compelled to do?

Was Hugh even under compulsion? I stared at a light blinking in a far distant part of the city. What if Hugh was doing this on his own accord?

There was no doubt that I needed to figure out how I could keep Hugh out of our business while still making him feel included. If his purpose was to pass along information to Portage, then I needed to feed him a few things to test that. I rested my head back against the headrest of my chair and closed my eyes.

As a newly mated female, my blood and body were craving his. I wanted to be back in my apartment, sating myself and my desires, but I didn't trust myself, and I sure as hell didn't trust Hugh. Newly mated couples had a hard time keeping their hands off one another, and even though I knew this was now a trap, my body didn't care.

As I saw it, I had a couple of choices. I could pretend I didn't know anything. Treat Hugh no differently, but watch him closely as he learned about our world, and I feed him intel slowly to see what happened with it. Or I could keep my distance until I needed him; that would effectually leave him in the dark and leave me stressed out from need and desire. My third choice was to break my mating with him by immediately mating with someone else—Clayton had offered. There was a fourth choice, but I wasn't sure I was ready to entertain that one yet. I could kill Hugh.

Killing him would be the easiest. I frowned, but it would also be a waste of potent blood—the blood of a reborn. My god, it had been incredible. My throat ached with the need for more, but I refused my craving. We didn't even have any idea what Hugh might be capable of doing. Killing him was off the table —for now.

I also didn't want to mate with Clayton, not right now—not ever if I didn't have to. He was a nice man, but I couldn't see myself falling in love with him or spending a hundred years with him at my side.

That left me with keeping this quiet and pretending every-thing was okay or keeping him at arm's length. I would have to be very careful around Joshua and Rex. If either of them found out that Hugh was planted here by Portage, they wouldn't hesitate to take him down.

For that reason alone, I realized that my only choice was to incorporate Hugh into my life and pretend all was well. I would have to feed him the intel that I wanted him to have. It would be tough, but I should be able to do that.

I would have to speak with Ryker and Conner too, and Angelina. Make sure they all knew that they had to be careful with what they said to him. Would they ask why? If they did, I would have to compel them to do as I say without question.

With the decision made, I forced thoughts of Hugh out of my mind and focused on field reports. From time to time, I would feel Hugh's emotions slip through our bond, but I tried to ignore them and make sure to keep my own emotions locked down.

Even though I wasn't paying close attention, I felt his humor, concern, lust, and intrigue. Part of me wanted to know what had caused each of those emotions, but another part knew better. I did not want to fall in love with Hugh, and this was the only way.

I felt them coming closer, knew they were about to join me in my office, and I locked down my mind even tighter. I didn't need my sister knowing any of this right now.

It took almost everything in me to stay still, and not rush into his arms, or let him take me over my desk as he wished he could. After I'd told Angelina to get him out of my office, I groaned.

I wasn't going to be able to deny my need for him. His blood was too strong, and our bond was surprisingly deep. If Hugh had been compelled, even he wouldn't know what he was doing. Would it be fair to blame him for something he wasn't even aware of?

I spent another hour working in my office but kept a part of my mind open to Hugh. He was still with my sister, and I had felt his lust for her more than once. Each time I wondered if he hadn't been compelled to be with me, would he have preferred to be with her. It wasn't just my sister that he lusted after, though.

No, Hugh McMurphy had already been a very sexual man before turned, and we had just jacked up his hormones. The man was going to be insatiable for a while. I stared at my computer; why was I here in my office alone, when I could be helping him sate those desires? Why did I deny myself something that I had wanted for so many years?

I glanced at the clock; the sun would be rising in a couple of hours. I had better get back to my mate before I raised any suspicions as to why I was away from him so soon after our mating.

I ran into Clay as I got off the elevator downstairs. "I was just coming to check on you. Everything alright?"

"Yes, everything is fine. I had a couple of things that needed urgent attention."

"Ah, work never stops, does it?"

"No."

"Well, if you need me to oversee anything during your honeymoon phase, just let me know."

I put my hand on his arm, feeling his generosity swelling under the surface. "Thanks, Clay. I'll let you know."

I was about to head into the lounge when Rex grabbed my arm, and Joshua was right behind me. "Why are you not with him?"

"I didn't know that I was required to be with him twenty-four seven," I replied dryly.

"No one leaves their new mate on their first night."

I laughed. "No one else is the mistress of the breed, Rex. I had work that required my attention." I put a hand on his shoulder and leaned closer. "I will let you in on a little secret, though. The night that Alex and I mated, he left me and went back to work thirty minutes later, and I didn't see him for two days. The night that I mated with your father, we were drugged, and we only had sex once, and then only two more times before we separated for a month. Not everyone needs to have twenty-four hours straight of sex and feeding."

He pursed his lips and frowned, and I smiled sweetly, patted his cheek twice, and then spun around and headed into the lounge.

Hugh was seated at the bar, laughing at something; he tapped his glass to Ryker's as they laughed harder. Around him were seven other people, all enjoying themselves, including my sister, who looked smitten with the man in front of her.

It was just after that thought registered in my mind that her eyes shifted from Hugh and landed on me. She straightened and frowned, probably because she hadn't realized that she had been leaning toward him suggestively. I was torn between not wanting to care and caring too much. I shouldn't care.

I smiled at her, letting her know that all was well, and Hugh's head snapped toward me. As soon as his gaze landed on me, I felt his lust rushing forward.

Ryker laughed and got up, moving away quickly. "And I think that's our cue to leave."

The rest of the group stood, and everyone began to head toward the doors. Hugh was still staring at me, and I glanced around to see the room empty as I stopped about five feet away.

"I'm sorry about breaking up the fun," I said.

He sipped from his glass, then set it on the bar before glancing around. "Where did everyone go?"

"They left us alone," I replied.

He stared at me hard, then let his gaze drift down my body and back up. "Are you done with work?"

"For now."

"Good," he said just before he lunged forward and wrapped his arms around my body. His lips crashed into mine, and I curled myself around him, enjoying the feel of his strong arms holding me. His mouth left mine, and he ran kisses down my neck. "Jesus, I want you so fucking bad right now, Kris."

"Then why don't we take this up to our apartment?" I suggested as I ran my hands over his back. While his lust was intense and new, mine wasn't far behind in the need-to-get-laid department.

"No, I can't wait," he growled into my ear as he groped at my breasts. His hands shifted to curl under my ass, and he lifted me. I wrapped my legs around his waist and squeezed.

CHAPTER TWELVE

HUGH

The moment my eyes landed on her, my desire exploded, and I couldn't hold back. I had to be buried deep in her.

I carried Kristin to a bench and shoved the table out of the way. Everything on it scattered to the floor, and the table dropped to the side. Kristin laughed as I reached behind my back and unlocked her legs. She stood in front of me, and it took everything in me not to tear her clothing from her body.

My hands shook as I tried to work her pants off her hips as she focused on my pants. I pushed her hands away to free myself, and she shimmied her pants off her legs. The minute she stepped out of them, I lifted her back up, and she centered herself over me. I spun us around and dropped to the bench behind me as I filled her. Her fangs latched on to my neck, and I was right behind her.

It took a little longer for us to hit that pinnacle, and I was glad because I was able to enjoy it this time. It still didn't last as long as I wanted it to, and I was no sooner done than I was ready to go again.

Kristin laughed as she caressed my face, still seated on my

lap. "Why don't we go up to our apartment so the employees can clean the lounge?"

"Our apartment?"

She spiked a sexy brow. "Well, we are mated now, right? I assumed you'd want to live with me."

"Do you want me to?"

She chuckled. "What I want is to get dressed and get back to our apartment so that I can enjoy you more in our bed. Let's go, and we can have this conversation later."

"Fine." I pulled her face to mine and kissed her passionately. Oddly enough, we hadn't kissed that much since we'd come together earlier. While I loved sucking from her neck, I did enjoy kissing her too. I needed to remember to do that more.

I helped her off my lap, and we got dressed in silence. I pulled her to me again and stared down into her blue eyes for a moment. She was beautiful, and I was lucky to have her now. I kissed her again, noting that she was also thankful as a warm feeling slipped through my chest. I laced our fingers together, bringing her hand to my lips and kissing it.

As we stepped out of the lounge, I found Ryker, Conner, Joshua, and Lorna standing off to the side.

"You can let the staff know they can close up for the night, and we won't be needing your services anymore tonight," Kristin stated as we walked past the group.

INSIDE THE ELEVATOR, Kristin put her thumb to a pad, and then the elevator began to move. I crowded Kristin into the corner. "I have another idea where I want to have sex with you."

She laughed. "Oh, really? Please don't tell me you want to have sex in the elevator."

I grinned. "Not tonight. Maybe another time."

"Okay, where?"

"On the roof."

She grinned. "You found my roof hideout, huh?"

I put my finger under her chin and lifted it so I could kiss her slowly. "Yes, I found your hideout, and I hope you will share it with me. I love the view, love being outside."

"You want to have sex on the roof?"

"Yes, I want to have you in front of me at the railing while I fuck you from behind. And while I do that, I want to drink from your neck and make you scream my name while you shatter around me."

My words were rough, dirty, and I wondered if she would be offended, but I felt her body begin to quiver, and her eyes shifted to a darker blue. "Well, then I think we need to get to the roof."

I pressed her against the wall, my erection hard and pulsing behind the fabric of my pants. I should have hit the stop button on the elevator and taken her right then.

But I didn't.

We kissed and groped one another while the elevator zipped up to the top floor. Once there, I lifted Kristin into my arms, and she laughed. "What are you doing?"

"I'm carrying you across the threshold. You got a problem with that?"

"Nope," she said and wrapped one arm around my neck. "I think it is a very nice gesture."

Inside her apartment, I wanted to head straight to the stairs, but I didn't. I forced myself to slow down. I eased her legs to the ground, keeping her body tight to mine as they touched. "How about we crack open a bottle of wine?"

She cocked her head. "You no longer in a rush to get me upstairs?"

I chuckled huskily. "Oh, I am, but I'm trying to be a gentleman here. I figured since we are mated, we'll be together for a little while. No need to rush anymore." I kissed her slowly. "Besides, if we don't make it up there tonight, there is always tomorrow, right?"

She wound her arms around my neck. "Very true. Why don't you pick out a bottle of wine, and I'm going to go change."

"Perfect," I whispered and kissed her nose.

While Kristin was changing, I scanned over the labels of her collection and found one of my favorites. I didn't drink real wine often—over the last few years it had become costly—but I did enjoy it when I could. I stood back and shifted my eyes over her bottles; there was a lot of money sitting here.

My gaze shifted around. The apartment was expensively decorated, too. How wealthy was she? Not that I cared about her money, but I was interested to know.

I went to the bar and dug around behind it until I found a corkscrew. Speaking of money, was I going to be able to go back to work? If I couldn't, what was I going to do? I couldn't live off of her financially; I had to do something to make money. Would they hire me at the VMF? Is that what it was called? I frowned as I uncorked the wine, realizing that there was so much that I didn't know.

When Kristin returned, she wore a long silk robe, and her thighs peeked out with each step. I held her wine glass out to her. She sniffed it. "Nice choice. Are you a wine connoisseur?"

I smirked and took a seat on the sofa. "I can't say that I drink it often, but I do enjoy a nice glass once in a while. I've had this before; it's good." Kristin stood there, watching me as if unsure of what to do.

"Can we talk for a little while?"

"Talk?" Her right eyebrow hiked sexily.

I chuckled. "Yeah, we don't seem to be able to do that very often before we tear each other's clothes off, but I would like to talk."

She slipped onto the couch, curling elegantly into the corner with her legs tucked under her. "Then we shall talk. What is it that you want to discuss?"

"Anything—everything," I replied with a chuckle.

She studied me for a moment. "I'm sure the topic of your job has been heavy on your mind." I nodded. "I don't think that you will be able to return to your job as you once did it, Hugh, but you can help us deal with them. The fact that you know them so well, and that you will be learning about us, will be beneficial. You do have to remember that you are one of us now. Your life is different, and we protect our way of life. Which means you are going to have to be careful with what you tell them."

"I understand that."

"And as for the other thing that was weighing heavily on your mind; I am very wealthy, most of us are. You will not need to make your own money, but I understand your need to provide. Eventually, you will amass your own fortune; it takes some time, be patient. For now, whatever you need is yours. I will get you set up with an account, and you can purchase what you want when you want it."

"How wealthy are you, Kristin?"

She smiled as she looked away. "The humans have a report that they put out yearly of the wealthiest humans. Let's just say that many of our breed would be on that list, me included."

My jaw dropped. "You're a billionaire?"

"Something like that, so like I said, you do not need to collect a paycheck. What is mine is yours. We are mated, so we share everything."

"Just like being married," I stated.

"Yes, just like being married. Does that bother you?"

I shook my head. "No. I don't think so. I never wanted to be married before, but—"

"But with me, it just feels right?" she asked, and I laughed.

"Does that sound stupid?"

"Not at all. I know you will have a lot to adjust to, but you will get there, and we will get things figured out. Eventually, you will find your place in our society, and we will have a better idea of what abilities you might have."

"Do you really think I will have abilities?"

Kristin leaned forward and put her palm out to me. "Touch me."

I pressed my palm to hers and felt our skin begin to warm. A slow glow emanated from our hands as heat moved up my arm. As it shifted higher, the hair on my arms began to stand on end, and I laughed softly.

Kristin's voice floated into my mind. *"Do you feel the power traveling through your body?"*

"Yes."

Our eyes locked over our hands, and I clasped her hand in mine. *"The glowing is us coming together. We are only barely touching, not trying to do anything, and yet we are glowing because we are focused on our touch."*

"Have you ever done this with anyone else?"

She shook her head slowly. *"No. This is our blood talking to one another, Hugh. Even if you can't do something else specifically, you can do this with me. You amplify my abilities, Hugh. You give me strength—a strength I will need to protect our breed and way of life."*

Her voice was so sexy as it whispered through my mind, and I began to pull her toward me. I set my wine glass down and removed hers before pulling her into my lap and kissing her. Our fingers still joined, the glow now becoming brighter as our passion flared.

I ran my mouth along her neck, and she whispered, "I thought you wanted to talk."

I grunted, "Talking is overrated."

She snickered as she shifted on my lap. "Let's go to the bedroom and talk in a different way."

* * *

THE NEXT EVENING I woke to an empty bed and silence in the apartment. I found coffee on in the kitchen, and after pouring myself a cup, I went to stand by the window. The door opened behind me, and I turned to find Clayton coming in with a female that I hadn't met before.

"Evening, Hugh, how are you feeling?"

"I'm feeling pretty damn good. What can I do for you?"

"Emily here needs to take a quick blood sample. We need it for your DNA on the computer system."

"Okay, easy enough," I said as I came forward and took a seat. Emily smiled at me, then set down a small package she'd been carrying with her and went about removing a needle, vial, and band to tie around my arm.

"Anything else that you find you are needing?" Clayton asked as Emily worked on preparing my arm.

"Not that I can think of, although do you happen to know where Kris is?"

"In her office. She starts working before the sun even goes down. Usually around four in the afternoon, she's at her desk and going through the news of the day. When the rest of the staff gets in around six, she already knows what needs to happen that day."

"Wow. Does Kristin do that all herself? I would think that she would have people to help her do that or do it for her?"

Clayton chuckled. "She does a lot of it herself. She's a bit of a control freak if you haven't already figured that out. Lainey, her assistant, and Garrett, her son, help her too."

I smirked. I had gotten the impression that she was a bit of a control freak, but with her position, I could imagine she would need that. "Glad to hear she lets people help her."

"I'm not so sure she lets them help, as they force her to allow them to help." He chuckled. "Speaking of Garrett, he's going to stop by soon to speak with you. I think Kristin wants you to work with him to flesh out ideas for your job."

"Wow, really? Okay, that would be good. I know I took a leave of absence from my job, but I was kind of just wondering what the hell I was going to be doing with my time for the next few weeks."

"Normally"—he glanced at me—"let's use a human marriage as an example, new couples spend a lot of time together in that first couple of weeks, but your mating is different than most. You have connected to the most powerful and busy woman of our breed. You do understand that, right?"

"Yes, I do."

"You are going to be spending a lot of time away from her, but we have people who will help you get acquainted with our life."

Emily picked up her things, nodded, and then quietly left. When she opened the door, Ryker stuck his head in. "Hey, big man! Garrett wants to know if you have time to talk."

"Perfect timing," Clayton said.

A younger man stepped around Ryker and grinned. We had met briefly before, but this was the first chance that I had to study him. He had a kind smile, long dark hair that hung around his shoulders with a slight wave to it, and bright-blue eyes.

He nodded as he approached. "Hugh, it's a pleasure to get a chance to speak with you finally. Already you have made a difference in my mother's life, which means a difference in the breed. I see good things happening because of the bond you have with my mother."

"I'm glad to hear that."

He smiled brightly for a moment, and then the smile vanished, and his eyes took on a ferocious glint that I never thought possible with him. "But if you do anything to hurt my mother, I will have you torn apart piece by piece."

CHAPTER THIRTEEN

ANGELINA

*M*y booted feet were kicked up on the desk, and I sipped from the mug that I had brought with me as I waited. My sister would be here soon. I could feel her coming. I yawned after I swallowed the brew, wishing that I hadn't been able to feel her so damn well. She had woken me up two hours earlier than I had intended.

While Kristin was good at blocking down her mind so that no one could get into her mind, she wasn't all that great at blocking how she felt. Since two this afternoon, she'd been awake, mentally wrestling with something significant. Was it Hugh? Had something happened?

Last night when she kicked us out of her inner sanctuary and told me to keep him away, I'd wondered what was going on. Was she concerned he would reveal too much to his task force? Or was there something else? After feeling her warring emotions for hours, I knew it had to be something more.

She could easily control the information that he received about the breed. Hell, she could compel him not to reveal information unless she approved it.

Had something gone wrong with the mating? I didn't think

so. Hugh hadn't been around anyone else, or done anything, so what else could be on her mind? And why had she gone to Joshua last night and demanded him to think about Alex's death? What did that have to do with mating with Hugh?

Hugh would have been only twenty-two years old when Alex died. Had Hugh lied about not knowing that he was a reborn? Did he have something to do with Alex's death? I was at a loss and about to drive myself nuts.

I stared at my boots, noticed a scuff on them, and frowned just as the door opened, and Kristin paused in the doorway and glared at me. "What are you doing in my office this early? You just get in?"

"No, I did not just get in. I am sitting here waiting patiently for you."

Kristin glanced away from me as she stepped into the room. "Why, and can you please get your feet off my desk?"

I raised a brow. "You are rather testy today, my dear sister. It must be the fact that you didn't sleep well last night. Your love life not as good as you anticipated?"

She stared at me, blinked once, and then looked away. "It's fine."

"And the feeding? Is it just as good?" I asked as I stood.

She came around the desk and took the chair I had vacated and then spoke. "It's fine also."

Fine? Did she really say it was just fine? "Who are you, and where is my sister?"

She looked at me like she was constipated. "What is wrong with you?"

"Me? What is wrong with me?" My voice got a little high-pitched. "Nothing! What I'd like to know is what the hell is wrong with you, sister dear."

"Nothing is wrong, Lena." She pushed a couple of buttons on a keyboard to bring up several virtual computer screens.

"Bullshit, Kristin!" I pushed her chair sideways so it

swiveled. "If nothing were wrong, you sure as hell wouldn't have been up hours ago, gnawing over something. You woke me up with your stress. So spill it."

"There is nothing to spill. It's just an adjustment."

I sat down on the edge of her desk. "Kristin, what's going on? Is there something wrong with Hugh? Are you just freaking out because you're mated again? Or is there something else going on?"

"Lena, it's nothing." She waved it away as she typed a few words and then hit the enter button.

"I can not leave it alone, Kris. Talk to me, damn it. Why don't you want Hugh around your office?"

She flopped back in her chair. "You're not going to leave me alone, are you?"

"No, so just spill it already before all the walls have ears."

She chuckled and glanced at the wall where I knew there was a clock.

"I saw something during the mating process."

My brows jumped. "You saw something?"

"Yes."

Oh, my god! She was like pulling teeth today. "What did you see? His penis? Because I'm pretty sure you had already seen that."

"No," she hissed. "I'm not talking about something physical. I saw a memory."

"A memory." I paused. "Did that memory have something to do with Alex's death?"

Her eyes snapped to mine. "Why would you ask me that?"

"Because I am well aware of the fact that you forced Joshua to think about it right after you mated to Hugh. He said something about you checking something. So what the hell were you checking?"

"It was nothing. I just needed to see the memory."

"Why? I seriously doubt you were feeling nostalgic after getting all hot and bothered with your mate."

She rubbed her temples. "Lena, I'm not in the mood right now."

I put my hand on her shoulder and lowered my voice. "Kris, talk to me. Tell me what's going on, please. You know I will do anything that I can to help."

"I need to do more thinking," she said softly.

"Tell me this, Kris. When you mated with him, you saw something in his mind, right?" She nodded as she stared at one of the screens. "And it was bad, right?"

"It wasn't great."

"Are you regretting your decision right now?"

A muscle in her jaw ticked for a moment. "No, I'm not. Hugh is going to be good for me, for us—the breed. I will figure out how to deal with this. I promise I'll talk to you about it soon, but until I figure out how to handle this, I need you to help keep him busy."

"What do you want me to do?"

"I don't know."

I pursed my lips. "Do you want him to start learning about us?"

"Yes, maybe you can get with Garrett and have him work with Hugh to teach him history and facts. You've had his blood, compel him not to share any of our history with anyone until I figure out what he can share."

"You want me to compel him? Why don't you do it?"

"I don't want to compel him if I don't have to. I need him to trust me, and if he finds out that I have compelled him, it might not go over very well. Just be subtle about it. Maybe more of a suggestion."

"Alright, I'll do that."

"On your way out, if you see Clayton, can you tell him to come here?"

And I'm dismissed. "Sure." Me and my coffee mug got off her desk and moseyed over to the door. "You sure you don't want to tell me anything else?"

"Yes, I'm sure. Give me some time to dwell over it, and after I figure it out, I'll share it with you."

"Share with me? You mean, you're going to let me join in on the fun with Hugh?" I smirked her way as she glared at me.

"Um, no. I'm keeping Hugh for a while, Angelina."

"Fine, but if you two get bored, just let me know."

"I'll keep that in mind."

I was going to say something else, but her attention was already back on the computers, and her eyes were skimming over the news headlines. Before I closed the door behind me, I studied my sister for a moment. No one else would notice the stress on her face, but I saw it. Something was really bothering her, and I wished she would let me in on it. Didn't she realize that two heads were better than one if you were trying to figure something out?

I headed down the hall, and as I approached the elevator, the door opened, and Clayton stepped out. "Ah, just the man I was looking for." He gave me a slight smile, which caused the scar on his left cheek to change shape and look slightly sinister.

"Why would you be looking for me?"

"Actually, I wasn't, the mistress was. She told me to let you know she needed to see you if I ran into you."

"I'm on the way to see her right now." We traded places, and I went to push the close door button. "How is she today? Everything go alright last night?"

I pursed my lips. "Yes, I think so. Something is bothering her, but I'm not sure what it is. As far as I know, things are good with them."

He nodded. "Alright, I'll talk to you later." He stepped back, and the doors started to close. I threw my hand out and stopped them.

"Clay," I called, and he turned.

"Did you get anything off of Hugh last night when you fed from him?"

He thought for a moment and then shook his head. "Nothing that stands out, why?"

I smiled brightly. "No reason. I'm just trying to figure him out."

He smirked. "Good luck with that, Lena."

The elevator doors closed, and I frowned at the back of them. So if Kristin saw something in Hugh's mind that bothered him, why didn't Clayton see it when he was practically draining him? He would have had a front-row seat to just about anything in Hugh's mind.

I headed up to the eighth floor and took the hallway down to Garrett's apartment. Since Garrett hadn't transitioned yet, sometimes he was up in the middle of the day doing things for the VMF or overseeing some of our day employees. If he wasn't in his apartment, I'd call him.

I knocked and waited. I was about to hit the door again when I felt his presence on the other side, but my nephew was not alone—interesting. The door pulled open, and I grinned at Garrett. "Hello, nephew."

"Aunt Lena," he chuckled. "What are you doing here so early?"

"I have a message from your mother, may I come in?"

He hesitated just the slightest bit, but then stepped back and pushed the door open. I grinned at him as I swooped past him and found Novah standing nervously in the living room.

"Well, hello there, Novah. A little early to be visiting, or have you been here long—like all day?" She looked slightly nervous as she glanced past me to Garrett.

"Hello, Angelina, I was just leaving."

"Please, don't cut your rendezvous short on my account,

although I do have a task for Garrett, so your plans would probably be cut short anyway."

She ignored me and stepped around the couch to avoid coming near me. "I'll talk to you later, Garrett."

"Bye." His wandering eyes followed her as she stepped out of his apartment.

"Well, I didn't expect that. I thought Novah was interested in your brother. I never expected her to rob the cradle."

Garrett frowned at me. "She isn't robbing the cradle; she came here to speak with me."

"Oh, really, Garrett? Is that why both of you have swollen lips and desire-filled gazes? And by the way, her zipper wasn't completely up on her pants."

He closed his eyes and inhaled deeply. "Can you just keep this between us?"

"Is there a reason this shouldn't be common knowledge? Other than the fact that she's over twice your age—not that age matters—but you haven't transitioned yet."

"We haven't said anything because I haven't spoken to Rex yet, and I don't want him finding out from someone else. He likes her."

"Are you sure about that, Garrett? I thought that Rex wasn't interested in Novah."

"What makes you say that?"

"Garrett, let me ask you a question. Did Novah approach you, or did you approach her?"

"Um, neither, we just started spending time together and hit it off."

"Be careful, Garrett. I'm not sure I trust her. She's very smart and a little conniving—kind of like me, which is why I noticed. I wouldn't put it past her to be trying to get into good graces to further her reach here."

"She wouldn't do that, Lena."

I laughed. "Oh, yes, she would. Novah is sneaky. Just make

sure that she is really into you and not what your status might one day be."

It wasn't long ago that news got out that Rex would not be the next one in line for the Master position. Ironic that Novah had decided to sink her hooks into the man who would one day be the new master.

"Look, can you not tell my mother about this?"

"I don't normally keep secrets from my sister." However, she was keeping shit from me—so one little one wouldn't hurt.

"I know, just for a little while. Let me figure this out, and if something is going on with Novah and me, I'll tell her and make sure Rex knows about it too."

"Fine, I'll keep it to myself—for now, but you need to do your mother a favor."

"What's that?"

"You need to work with her new mate. Start teaching him about our world and about our breed."

He shrugged. "Okay, easy enough."

"What do you think of him?"

He sat down and kicked his bare feet up on the coffee table. "To be honest, I have no real thoughts on him—yet. I haven't spoken more than ten words to him. Let me work with him for a little while, and then I'll let you know."

"Alright, let me know what you think."

He eyed me carefully. "What do you think about him?"

Well, I sure as hell couldn't say that I thought he was yummy. "I think he will be good for your mom. I'm looking forward to seeing what he'll be able to do in the future and how he can help her."

"If this works, are you going to start searching for your own reborn mate?"

"Maybe."

"You know, I was kind of wondering if Mom's blood is so

different—and yours too—do I have any difference in my blood since I'm her son?"

"I don't know, Garrett, but that might be something that we should look into."

"I have thought about that a few times, but Rex doesn't seem to be special in any way."

"Oh, Rex is special, but you're right, not like his mom. He's much more like his father." Pushy and rigid in his thoughts, I continued to myself.

CHAPTER FOURTEEN

JOSEPH

"Show him in," I said to Melinda as she stuck her head into my den. I put my papers away and came from around my desk as the door opened and in walked a tall man with light-brown hair. He was younger than I expected, but I knew he had been turned young.

"Gabriel, it is a pleasure to meet you in person."

"You too, sir," he said as he approached me.

"Have a seat."

I poured us a drink, not even asking if he wanted one, and then handed it to him. He immediately put it to his lips and then smiled. "That is a fine whiskey."

"Yes, it is. One hundred years, the best that you can get. They knew how to make good whiskey back then, none of that fake shit that they make now."

Gabe chuckled slightly. "Yeah, things have changed."

I smirked at him. "So I have heard of you. I understand that you used to be very close to the mistress."

"Yes, for years we were thick as thieves."

"And when did that change?"

"About two years ago. Kris got pissed with my mate, Olivia, and banished her."

"Isn't your mate a human-turned?"

"Yes."

"Isn't that when she changed her laws to say that no more human-turned could be made?"

"Yeah, that is exactly when and why."

"You haven't spoken to her since?"

"Hell, no! Olivia was her best friend, but Kris just kicked her to the curb because she had a little too much fun one night."

"What do you mean, a little too much fun?"

He shifted in his seat as if he were nervous. "Olivia gets into these phases where she can't always control her appetite."

"Ah, so she feeds a little too often?"

"Yeah, and she's not one to stop when she starts, so she's left a wake of bodies behind her. Kris got really pissed after she almost showed up on the front page."

"That's why she sent your mate away? Did she send you away too?"

"No, but I wasn't going to stay there when she sent Livy away. I love her."

"Did you not love Kristin?"

"Yeah, like a sister, but we all know that you don't always get along with your siblings, right?" Gabe chuckled darkly.

I joined him. "That is very true. You haven't spoken to her since? Kristin, I mean."

"Nope, not once, and I have no intention of doing so either. I'm furious at how quickly she turned her back on us just because Olivia was a little reckless."

"She wasn't reckless; she was living up to her species. Don't you think that we should all be able to feed on humans whenever and wherever we want?"

Gabe laughed. "Wouldn't that be great."

"Of course, that would be great. That is our true nature, our destiny! That is what I am trying to do, Gabriel."

"I know, and that's why I've been trying to help the cause."

"You have been doing very well, at least that's what I hear."

"Thank you, sir. I know I don't know much about you, but she doesn't belong in that position. She can't handle it. I'm sure you would do a much better job."

"I appreciate your support." I sipped from my glass. "Gabriel, were you not best friends with Julian Hutchinson?"

He frowned and glanced down as he swallowed. "Best friends, sir. I wasn't there when he died. I wish I were. Did you know him?"

"Not then, I didn't."

"Sir? What do you mean by not then?"

"What if I told you that Julian is alive, only not as Julian."

I could hear his heart beating faster with excitement. "Are you serious? But how?"

"Like the mistress, Julian has come back as a reborn."

"What? Where is he? Who is he?"

"You have already met him, my son."

Gabriel's mind spun, and after a brief few seconds, calmed and then closed off from me. I studied him carefully, wondering why he had closed his mind, but not daring to ask as I didn't want him to know I was listening so carefully.

"Zander? Zander is Julian?"

"Yes. Does that surprise you?"

He rubbed his jaw for a second as he looked around, and then his mind began to open again. An image of him and Julian standing in a room watching a woman with short, strawberry-blond hair. Julian and Gabe smiled at one another, and I felt the camaraderie and friendship they shared as the woman turned and laughed at them. The mistress looked much different back then. The memory changed, and it was of Gabe staring at Julian, noting his eyes.

117

"They have the same eyes. I noticed that the night we had dinner. Olivia said he smelled like Julian, but I didn't notice it."

"Ah, I wasn't aware they might smell the same," I replied.

"How do you know that he's Julian? Has he told you that?" Gabe seemed very excited by this news now, and his mind was opening and closing as if he wasn't able to control it.

"Let's just say that I have someone who works for me that can sense these things and help me figure them out."

He looked confused for a moment. "Does he know?"

I shook my head. "No, I have worked very hard to keep this knowledge from him. It is all part of my plan to get to the mistress and take my rightful position."

He frowned. "You are going to use him against Kristin?"

"Well, maybe use is the wrong word. I want to entice him to get to know her."

He frowned. "But how will that help you get to your rightful place?"

I chuckled. "All in good time, Gabriel. What I would like to know is if you would be willing to help me."

"What can I do?"

"Well, it is time for Zander to remember his previous life, but I don't want to be the one to tell him. He's been sheltered from it for years. Laura watches out for him and removes memories that he might bring forward. Now it's time to allow those to come forward."

"What can I do to help?"

"Casually speak to him, maybe bring up a memory he might have, or mention the mistress. I understand from Laura that he has quite a fascination with her already. I have a feeling it will only take a few conversations with him before the memories come forward, and he realizes that something is going on."

"I guess I can do that. Is there anything else you want me to do?"

"Not right now, let's just get his mind to open, and once he realizes what's going on, you and I will talk again."

"Alright, sir. I can do that."

"Excellent, Gabriel. The mistress might not understand how important you and your mate are, but I sure do. You two will have a place in my organization."

"Thank you, sir." Gabe threw back the rest of his whiskey and grinned.

"Fantastic, Gabriel. Now you will *want* to forget that we met face-to-face. You will *want* to remember our conversation, but think that it happened over the phone. You *want* to leave now and find a way to speak with Zander soon."

"You have a good day, sir." Gabe stood immediately and began to leave.

After he left, I continued to sit there and think about him. He seemed very willing to help out. Was he up to something? Or was he just excited to have his old friend back, and maybe, just maybe stick it to the mistress?

CHAPTER FIFTEEN

KRISTIN

"*I*'m surprised that you are in your office so early. I figured you might be late tonight, or not come down at all." Clayton grinned as he stepped in.

I smiled at Clayton as I leaned back in my seat, waving my computer screens away for a few minutes. "Yeah, well, I guess it was just another run of the mill mating."

He barked out a laugh and took a seat. "Run of the mill? Damn, Kristin, if you think mating to Hugh was run of the mill, you probably would have thought mating with me would have been snoozeville."

I chuckled. "That's not what I meant. I meant because it's not new to me, you know that old adage, been there, done that, got the t-shirt?"

"Yeah, I remember that saying."

"Yes, well, with four matings under my belt, this one was just another business arrangement." I frowned. "Come to think of it, my last one was too."

"Hey, at least you loved Alex."

"True, I did," I admitted.

"Think you can love Hugh?"

I shrugged. "Only time will tell, but I didn't mate with him to find love. I mated with him for the power, and I'm not afraid to admit that to you."

He snickered. "Only me?"

"For the moment," I replied.

He studied me carefully. "How did things go last night?"

"They went off without a hitch, if that's what you mean."

"Why do I feel like you are holding something back, Kristin?"

Clayton had been working with me for years, and I had come to trust his judgment. That's why I had asked him to turn Hugh in the first place. If there was anyone I could talk to, it was him.

"Clay, when you were turning him, did you get anything odd off of him? Did you see anything that might have caused you concern?"

His eyes blinked quickly for a minute, and his brow furrowed slightly, causing the scar on his left cheek to shift slightly. I had always thought that his scar added something to his sex appeal.

"No, I don't think so, Kristin. I purposely tried to shift through many of his thoughts to make sure, but other than a few small roadblocks, his mind was pretty open—and boring. Holy crap, his life has been work, work, and more work. However, I did see the dream that he mentioned about his great-grandfather dying. It was a brutal death."

"You noticed a few roadblocks?"

"Yeah, why? Did you see something?"

"I don't know," I replied softly. "If you didn't see anything, I wonder if I'm making things up. Perhaps I'm trying to keep myself withdrawn a little bit so that I don't get too attached for fear of the unknown."

"Damn, Kristin, I think that's the last thing that you should do. I think you should be exploring what the two of you have. Maybe you can figure out if he has a special ability."

"We glow," I stated.

His left brow popped a little higher. "You glow? You showed us that when you announced your mating. Is this glow different now?"

"When we touch, when we are focused on each other, touching, our skin glows slightly. If we focus, we can make it brighter. We don't need Angelina to do it now."

"And you have never done that before?"

"Not without help. I mean, Angelina can sometimes give me a sheen if I'm trying, and when Julian used to connect with us, I could get a slight glow, especially to my eyes, but Hugh and I aren't even trying. It just happens."

"That just shows you how powerful he is and how he will complement you so well."

"You think so?"

"Yeah, I do. I think you should stop worrying and see what you two have between each other. I think you have so much stress on you right now that you see shadows where there are none. Take a step back, enjoy some time with Hugh, and refresh yourself. It's quiet right now; take advantage of that. Maybe you and Hugh can do a night out on the town."

"I'm not sure Hugh wants to do that until he tells his job what's going on. He did take a leave of absence."

"Ah, that's true. Well, stay in then, but get out of here, and spend some time with him. Tell him about our world."

"I'll think about it. In the meantime, I need you to do me a favor first, Clay."

"What's that?"

"I need you to find Emily and get a blood sample from Hugh. I don't know why I never thought about studying our DNA, but I want his compared to mine and my sister's, along with about a dozen other people, both transitioned and not."

"What are you thinking?"

"I'm wondering if there is a way to tell earlier if someone is a reborn or not."

"Wow, that would be huge."

"Wouldn't it? If we could somehow test the human population or those we perceive to be human, then we might find more of us out there."

"And if we do?"

"Then we use that, Clay. Can you imagine how powerful we would be with five, ten, twenty reborns with us?"

"You think that there might be that many of them out there?"

I laughed. "Clay, I do. I think there are a lot of us out there, and I want to find them. Help them!"

"Alright, I'll find Emily and have her get a sample from him."

"Don't tell him what it's for."

"I won't. I'll tell Hugh that we just need it for our records."

"Good idea and pick other people to test. Let's get at least twelve, or maybe we should do twenty."

"Twenty will be good. Hell, Kris, why don't we just run everyone here and start a DNA database."

"You know that's not a bad idea. It could help us tie people together."

"It might tell us a lot," he stated. "Well, let me go round up Emily and get working on this."

"Thanks, Clayton."

He paused by the door. "What made you think of doing this in the first place, Kris?"

I inhaled slowly and thought over my words for a moment. While I trusted Clayton, I wasn't sure I was ready to divulge my real reason. "I'm trying to figure out the best way to win the war, Clayton."

"Alright then, I'm on your side. I'll get working on it, and you finish up in here and get back to your mate. Take some time off;

I'll cover for you, and if something comes up, you know that I will reach out to you."

"Thank you, Clayton."

Shortly after Clayton left, I went back to the news to see if there was anything that I needed to know. I was about to clear my desk and take Clayton's advice when my desk phone rang.

I clicked the button, and an image popped up above the phone. "Hello, Jacques."

He grinned. "My dear Kristin, I hear that congratulations are in order, but I didn't expect you to answer your phone, mon amour."

"You know me, Jacques, I love my work."

"Oui, but more than you love having sex and binge-feeding? I think not." He laughed. "You work too hard; American people have always worked too hard."

"I do, I know I do, but a lot is going on. You are up early."

"Or I am up late, depends on how you look at it. I was just finishing up with some things and didn't want to miss out on congratulating you. Is it true what I heard; your new mate is a reborn?"

"Wow, news travels fast. It is true," I replied.

"Ah, the powerful Mistress is even more powerful now. You took him rather quickly to your bed, not that I fault you. I couldn't get you to mine fast enough."

"Time was not on his side, and I don't recall having sex with you in a bed. I believe our first time was the pool, then the deck, and then the shower."

He chuckled. "You know what I mean, mon amour. Well, I look forward to meeting him. What is his name?"

"His name is Hugh McMurphy. He's a third-generation reborn from Galen Donahue; he's his great-grandson."

"Third-generation? Est-ce possible? Did you say Galen's great-grandson?" He whipped through something in French too quickly for me to catch it. "That is amazing. Fantastique! I knew

Galen, he was a good man, not very focused, but a good man all the same. Loved to fish—isn't that what killed him?"

"Yes, it did."

"Well, this is all quite a remarkable catch, Mistress."

I chuckled. "Thank you, Jacques."

"I hope that you intend to invite us all over to meet the new master?"

I tried not to bristle at that. "When the time is right, I will invite everyone to join in my celebration."

"Of course, you will. We must see this third-generation reborn with our own eyes." He paused. "Although I might have to speak with him soon. I do not understand how any new mate of yours could let you out of his sight this early."

I laughed. "I had something to get done, and he is being entertained. I was about to head back to him."

"Well, do not let me keep you. Go, enjoy your new time together, feed well. I know it must be incredible to have someone to share that with again."

"That is true, Jacques." We said our goodbyes, and I ended the call, the image vanishing into thin air.

Damn, I didn't even think about what everyone outside of here was going to think—or say. I fled my office before another call could come in and paused at Lainey's office to leave her a note saying I was not to be disturbed today and to speak with Clayton if anything was needed.

A few minutes later, I was stepping off the elevator as Josh was stepping out of his apartment.

"Where have you been?" he asked, glancing at the closing door of the elevator.

"I was in my office taking care of business."

"Why didn't you tell me?"

"Because I am quite capable of going to my office alone, Josh. Now, I'm going to my apartment, and I plan on being busy for the rest of the night, so you will need to find something else to keep you busy."

"I can—" he started to say, and I held my hand up.

"You can go away, is what you can do. I do not need you hovering in the hallway. I will be safe with Hugh, and after feeding, I am stronger and more alert than I have been in a very long time."

"Alright," he said softly, and I didn't miss the irritation in his eyes. I hadn't said that to hurt him, but to let him know I would be safe on my own. Not that I was going to be alone.

I rubbed my hand down his arm. "I'll see you tomorrow. Why don't you check in with Clayton and see if he needs anything."

"I will do that, Mistress."

I nodded and headed to my apartment. When I stepped in, I paused as I took in my son and my mate sitting at the table watching something on a virtual screen.

Hugh's face snapped my way, and I saw the fierceness in his blue eyes as the scent of my blood hit him. He held himself with great restraint as he stood slowly. "Hi, I didn't expect to see you for a while."

My son turned. "Oh, hey, Mom. You need something?"

I kept my eyes locked on Hugh. "Yeah, I need you to leave, Garrett."

From the corner of my eye, I saw Garrett look between the two of us and heard his chuckle before he grabbed his things. "I'm out of here. Just let me know when you come up for air. I wanted to talk to you about something."

That got my attention, and I turned to him. "Anything important?"

"Nothing that can't wait a little while." He smiled, and while I saw stress in his eyes, I knew that what he said was true. It would wait.

"I'll speak to you later."

"See you later, Hugh." Garrett kissed my cheek. "Mom."

My gaze had gone back to Hugh, and I felt the build of the sexual tension rising in both of us. The minute the door clicked closed, I stepped forward slowly. Hugh remained where he was, maybe unsure of how to respond to me.

I paused in front of him. "I owe you an apology."

Lines marred his forehead. "For what?"

"For mating with you and then practically disappearing —twice."

"Kristin, I know you have an important job." I put my fingers up to his lips.

"My job is important; the breed is important, but you are now my mate, and that makes you just as important. I have not given you the time and attention that you deserve. I would like to rectify that."

The lines faded, and a slow sexy smile filled his face. "Yeah, and how do we rectify that?"

I took his hand and pulled him to the couch. "Have a seat."

He sat down, and then I went to my knees; his nose flared as I reached for the buckle on his pants and began to undo it. Hugh's fingers twitched, but otherwise, he didn't move until I needed to shift his pants off his hips.

Right before I took him into my mouth, I stared up at him, letting my gaze soften. "Let me show you what it really means to be mated."

CHAPTER SIXTEEN

ZANDER

*L*aura had asked me to meet her and a few friends for dinner. When I arrived at the boardwalk where she told me to meet her, she wasn't there. I leaned on the railing and glanced around, noticing a man sitting on a bench facing the beach. He was one of Laura's friends; what was his name? Gabe?

He shifted his face toward me, and after our eyes locked, he hesitated only a second before he smiled and lifted his hand in greeting. I glanced around to see if Laura was anywhere, but didn't see her, so I went to say hello to him.

"It's Gabe, right?" I asked as I reached him.

"Yeah, Zander, right?"

"That's right. Are you waiting for your mate? I'm sorry, I forgot what her name was."

"Olivia, yeah, she's with Laura. They are shopping. I was sent away and told to wait for you."

I chuckled. "Women and their shopping."

"Exactly," Gabe replied drolly and scooted over so I could take a seat on the bench too. "How are you doing?"

"I guess I'm fine, you?"

"About as good as I can be." He paused. "I'm not a beach person. I prefer to live inland, visit lakes and such."

I smirked his way. "So why do you live near the beach?"

He rolled his eyes my way. "Olivia."

I chuckled. "The things we do for women."

"Oh, yeah, man, I have known some guys that have bent over backward for the women they care about."

I nodded. "Yeah, well, not me."

"Ha! Not me either. I had a friend, he was my best friend, and man, he was so crazy in love with this woman that he just let her walk all over him. He couldn't get her out of his head."

I glanced his way. "Did you talk some sense into him?"

"No, eventually he realized that he needed to get away from her, restart his life."

"Did he get a fresh start?"

"He did. He met another woman, and eventually, he and the woman that he had loved for like forty years became friends again."

"Well, that's good for him." I stared out over the beach, wondering why the hell we were talking about this. "He still with the new woman? Still happy?"

Gabe grew quiet. "No, he's dead. Julian and Lyssa were killed in an attack about thirty-five years ago."

My face whipped toward his. "What did you say?"

Gabe's face was expressionless. "I said they were killed about thirty-five years ago."

"What were their names?"

"Lyssa and Julian."

Julian. Julian. Julian. The name echoed through my mind with each beat of my heart. "Gabe, what was the name of the woman that he loved?"

Gabe opened his mouth to speak but closed it just as Laura and Olivia joined us. "Hey, ladies, did you get all your shopping done?"

Olivia kissed him before he stood. "We did. What were you guys talking about?"

I stood abruptly, not wanting Gabe to share our conversation. "We were complaining about how women love to shop so much."

"Oh, please," Laura said with a laugh. "You love to shop, too."

"Um, no, not really."

"Then why do we constantly have packages delivered to our house?"

"Because I'm bored," I told her, and everyone laughed.

"Yeah," Olivia spoke up. "And I'm starved, so let's go eat."

For the next two hours, we relaxed, and I found that I really enjoyed their company. Olivia was wild and had no filter when it came to speaking her mind, and while Gabe was quieter, he was still great company.

We ended up at a club after dinner and danced until the wee hours of the morning. Several more of Laura's friends joined us, and before long, it was like we were in the center of a huge party. I was enjoying myself more than I had in a while, and it wasn't until the place was starting to quiet down a little bit that Gabe came to my side again.

"You asked me a question earlier, and we got interrupted."

"Yeah, what question was that?" I knew, but I didn't want him to think that I'd been mulling it over all night. There was no reason for him to believe that the name Julian meant anything to me. The fucked-up thing was, I had no idea why that name *did* mean anything to me.

"You asked what the woman's name was. The woman that Julian loved above all else."

"Ah, yeah, I did." I grinned. "Forgot about that conversation," I said with a chuckle.

Gabe grinned, but it was almost like he knew I was lying. "Julian was in love with a woman named Kristin."

For a moment, nothing else existed. Just the two names that

swirled through my mind, Julian—Kristin—Julian—Kristin —Julian.

Pain sliced through my skull. My hands flew to the sides of my head as images flickered in hyperspeed. I swore that right then, my skull was going to explode as two voices began a dialogue inside the turmoil of my mind, and I was helpless but to listen.

"Julian, I know you were hurt and angry, but I also know that what you said wasn't true. You don't hate me. Yes, I know I hurt you, and I took advantage of your feelings—more than once—but you can't hate me."

"Why the hell not?"

"Come on, Julian, I know you can't hate me. I love you, Jules; you know that."

"Your words mean nothing, Kris. Did you seriously think that you could come all the way out here, tell me you love me and miss me, and I'd come back to you? That I'd return to watch you live your life with someone else? You've fucking lost your mind."

"Zander?" A hand clamped on my shoulder, and it took everything to yank myself out of my own mind and focus on Gabe. "You alright, man? Where'd you go?"

"Yeah." I dropped my hands. "I'm fine, just got a weird headache, that's all." I glanced around and realized that the music was way too loud, and the lights were flashing so fast that they made me dizzy. Or maybe that was the words that had been spinning around in my mind. What the fuck? "If you'll excuse me, I think I'm going to split. Will you let Laura know I headed out?"

"Yeah, sure, man. You sure you're okay? You kind of look like you saw a ghost."

I swallowed tightly. "Yeah, I'm fine. Night, Gabe."

I practically ran from the club and began to suck in lungful's of air as I hit the boardwalk again. I clenched my hands around the railing as another vivid scene exploded into my mind.

A woman with mostly red hair and some blond highlights was lying in a puddle of her own waste; her stomach was enlarged with child, but she lay motionless. I could practically feel the fear coating my gut for the person who was viewing the scene. Words were hollow, echoes of murmurs as he moved around her, pulling her dirty shirt off and trying to get her to feed. I saw her face, recognized it instantly, and felt my knees buckle as her face disappeared into the neck of the man in my vision.

A memory? Was it a memory? Was I remembering this? Husky words roared through my mind again. *"I'm here, baby. I'm so sorry. I'm so damn sorry for what I said. I didn't mean it; you were right; I didn't mean it, baby. I love you, Kristin. I will always love you."*

A shiver racked me so hard that I almost went to my knees, and I tried to shut down my mind. I forced the image out. Trying to shove them behind a wall, but more and more kept crashing down.

Images of a house, a car, that same lake that I had seen several times, and a dog. Sounds of laughter and shouts, whispers of love, dreams, a future. It took everything in me to get into a transport and get back to the house. When I arrived, I went straight to the shower and stood under the spray, my hands flat on the tile wall, my head hanging down as I was bombarded with thoughts, images, tastes.

What the hell was going on? What was wrong with me?

Her face kept coming back to me, sometimes serious, sometimes in joy, but every single time it settled into my vision, I felt something around my heart tighten. How could I know her? How could I feel this about her? She was the opposite of what I believed. She ruled over part of the breed that I did not belong to.

How could I possibly know so much about the Mistress? How was it possible for this to be real? How long ago was this?

Didn't Gabe say something about Julian dying thirty-five years ago? Jesus, I was thirty-five. How had I gotten his memories? I turned the water off and got out of the shower, wiping the steam from the mirror with a towel. I stared into the blurry image.

Was I Julian?

CHAPTER SEVENTEEN

HUGH

When Kristin said she was going to show me what it meant to be mated, she wasn't kidding. The two of us had sex on every surface of the apartment. The only people that came in were waiters who were delivering food. No one else even knocked on the door. We had also shared so much blood that I swear I was more her than me now.

When we weren't having sex, Kristin was asking me about my life and sharing information about hers. We talked a lot about life as a human and not knowing about the world. It was ironic that we had both grown up not knowing what we really were but knowing that we were different than others. I think that connected us in a much deeper way.

After two days, the intense need to have her constantly had begun to wane. Not that I didn't still want her every second, but it wasn't a constant aching need like it had been the day she had come to me and told me things were about to change.

We were lying on the couch, having just finished watching a movie, when she spoke softly. "After we mated, I kind of freaked out a bit. I'm sorry about that."

I chuckled as she rolled to her back so that she could see me better as I was lying behind her against the back of the couch. "Yeah? I wasn't sure what to expect, so I guess I didn't notice. I thought you were normal, and I was a freak."

She shook her head and touched the side of my face with her fingertips. "You are far from a freak, Hugh. What we have shared in the last few days is normal."

"What made you freak out, Kristin?"

"Honestly?"

I touched the tip of her nose. "Always, Kris. No matter what you need to say, I want you to be honest, even if I won't like it."

"I will try."

"I hope you do."

She sighed. "I think it was because it had been so long since I'd been mated to someone, that I got scared. The last man I mated with was Alex, and I knew him almost as well as I knew myself. I didn't know anything about you, not really, and even though I knew it was a smart move, it scared me because it's a big deal."

"It is a big deal. You're not scared now, are you?"

"No." She smiled widely. "No, I think we are going to have a good relationship. I believe that once your body and mind calm down a bit, we'll be able to figure out more about you and see what you can do."

"So, you just want to use me for my body and mind, huh?" I chuckled.

"Is that a problem?" she said seriously and then started to laugh. "And no, I am kinda getting attached to the rest of you, especially your very sexy mind and kind heart."

I stared at her and felt my chest warm. I had been fascinated with her since I first laid eyes on her; now, I felt more. Over the last two days, we had begun to build a stable relationship. I didn't love her, but I could see myself falling for her.

"Can I ask you a question?"

"Sure."

"Do you think you could fall in love with me?"

She didn't even hesitate before she responded, "Yes. Do you?"

"Yeah, I think I can. I feel a lot with you. I like how it feels, and after spending this time with you, I feel a lot more secure in my decision to not only join the race but to mate with you. You know that you weren't the only one who was nervous about this whole mating."

"Yes, I know that. I should have been more sympathetic to that."

"It's okay; I think you made up for it." I cupped her cheek and pulled her in to kiss her slowly.

"As long as you have forgiven me."

"Absolutely." I studied her. "When do we have to go back to reality?"

"Sadly"—she laughed and sat up—"in about fifteen seconds."

"Wow, that fast, huh?"

"Clayton is on his way up. He's just getting off the elevator." She headed toward the door as I sat up, glad that I was at least wearing clothes.

She opened the door. "Come in, Clayton."

"Is everyone decent?"

"Yes, for once," she called over her shoulder as she came back to the couch and curled herself into the corner. Close enough for me to touch, but just far enough away to put distance between our bodies. I already missed the feel of hers against mine.

"I'm glad that you took some time off; both of you look like you put that to good use," Clayton said with a chuckle. "Of course, everyone on this floor decided to sleep in other rooms for the last two days."

My eyes snapped to Kristin as she laughed. "We weren't that bad."

Clayton snickered. "Yes, you were."

"What are you talking about?" I asked them.

"Our connection is powerful, Hugh, and our desire is a bit overwhelming. Others can feel it, and it affects them, too."

"Oh," I replied dumbly. "So we were turning everyone on, huh?"

"Yes, just a bit," Clayton replied.

"Awesome," I snickered.

Kristin rolled her eyes at me playfully. "So, what is going on out there in the world? I'm assuming that something happened if you came here to speak with me."

Clayton flicked his eyes toward me. "Yes, but it's of a delicate nature."

I stood. "And that's my signal to give you all a little privacy."

"Actually, Clayton, let's go up to the patio and talk for a few minutes. I could use some fresh air. Hugh, why don't you shower and get dressed. Maybe you can work with Garrett for a while tonight to learn more of your ancestry history. I'm going to need to head into my office for a little while."

"Okay, I'll do that." When Kristin stood, she came to me, and I leaned down and kissed her tenderly.

"I'll see you later," she said, and then they headed toward the stairs. I wished that she would talk in front of me, but I understood that I was still an unknown to her.

I showered, dressed, checked my work email, and was in the kitchen getting a drink when Clayton came down from the roof thirty minutes later.

"How are you doing, Hugh? Any questions?"

"No, I think so far, I'm doing alright. Kristin answered a lot of questions for me over the last couple of days."

"That's good. You let me know if you need anything, alright?"

"I will."

"Kris asked if you could come up to the roof."

"Sure, thanks, Clayton."

"You're welcome." I watched him leave and wondered why Kristin wanted me to come up there. I wasn't going to find out until I went, so I headed up the stairs. As I reached the landing, I turned to find her standing at the balcony naked.

Instant hard-on.

Kristin turned her head to the side, her long dark-red hair such a contrast to the alabaster skin as it hung down her back, and a few strands floated up in the air current.

I whipped my shirt over my head and tossed it to the side as I approached her. I went directly to her, wrapping my arms around her waist and putting my face to her neck. "I'm hoping this is for me, and you weren't dressed like this for Clayton."

"Oh, no, I remember you telling me that you wanted to have sex here. I figured it was a good way to finish up our little reprieve."

"Oh, fuck yeah," I growled into her neck as I ran my hand down her stomach and between her legs.

It was almost hard to believe with all the sex we'd had these last two days that I could want more, or that the equipment would work. As a human male at the age of forty, having sex twice in a night was a feat in itself.

Kristin widened her stance so I could feel her better. After a few minutes of teasing her, I removed my pants and was back behind her. I stared over her shoulder into the city as I entered her from behind. My hand wrapped around her neck to hold her face away as I slid my fangs into the soft flesh of her neck.

Kristin whimpered as I continued to draw from her, while I rocked into her from behind. It was that moment that I suddenly realized something.

I was at the top of the world, the top of the food chain. I was important now, and I was going to live forever. The most important person in this new world belonged to me. She was gloriously mine, body and soul, and I swore that I would earn her heart too. I was going to do everything I could to keep her at my side and enjoy the position beside her.

Maybe one day soon, I could help her rule, and not just assist her when she needed my strength.

Kristin hit the pinnacle and pulled me over the top as she clenched around me. I squeezed her breast as I drew one final time from her neck and scanned the city. Was there anyone out there watching us?

In that instant, I felt someone behind me, and I knew who it was without turning. I could feel Angelina almost as well as I could feel Kristin. Their shared blood sang in my veins.

Angelina hadn't expected to walk in on us like this, and I wondered why she hadn't turned to leave. I released Kristin's neck, licked the puncture marks, and turned to look over my shoulder.

How long had she been there? Long enough to see us hit that glorious orgasm? I'm pretty sure she had. I kissed Kristin's neck. "We have company."

"I know," she said softly.

I turned from Kristin, then stepped toward my pants while keeping my eye on Angelina. She brazenly let her gaze drift down my body, hover on my groin area, and then return to my face. There was no way not to notice the desire shining toward me. It made me hard all over again.

"You need something, Lena?" Kristin asked as she reached for the long cotton t-shirt that she'd been wearing.

"Sorry, hadn't expected to walk in on that," she said brightly as she turned away from me.

"You could have joined us," I whispered toward her, and she nailed me with a what-the-fuck look briefly.

"Keep dreaming," she replied softly.

I chuckled as I began to walk toward her. She kept her gaze off of me and focused on her sister. "I'll give you ladies a few minutes to speak. I think I require another shower."

As I went down the stairs, I wondered about my lusting thoughts for Angelina. Was it because she shared Kristin's blood? Or was there something else about Angelina that called to me?

It didn't matter. I was with Kris, and I was going to be with her for a long time.

CHAPTER EIGHTEEN

ANGELINA

I should have walked away. Should have left as quietly as I came, but I didn't. My sister and Hugh were deep into it as I came upon them on the patio, and the sight in front of me mesmerized me.

The two of them stood against the railing, completely nude, with only the city lights behind them lighting the area. The way they moved was as if they had been together for years, and not merely a few days. The sounds they made, the mixture of their scents, sweet and smoky, it all made me slightly dizzy.

I both loved and hated it. It was pleasure and pain, and I wanted to run away, but I was frozen in place and had to watch. The worst part of it was that they both knew I was there. My sister way before Hugh, but they knew I'd seen at least a little bit of it.

It made me jealous as hell, but I didn't have time for that, or for the proposition that Hugh was giving. Not that I would have taken him up on it if I had the time. Okay, so maybe part of me really wanted to take him up on it, but only a part. That small devious part that liked the thrill of doing things I shouldn't, and having sex with my sister's mate might have been at the top of the list next to don't get staked or go out in the sun. All of them seemed to fit into the category of self-preservation. That was something I had not developed until after Kristin and I mended fences and grew closer.

I'd seen what my sister was like when she'd lost her patience with someone. Her best friend, Olivia, had been the perfect example. Kristin had tried to cover up some of her indiscretions, and by indiscretions, I meant random human kills. Kristin had overlooked a few, but when a front-page headline showed almost enough of Olivia in the photograph to be recognizable to the public, Kris had lost her shit.

The two of them had gotten into a screaming match, nose to nose where taunts were thrown about Olivia being a raging beast, and Trent had been right, to Olivia screaming back about Kris being all high and mighty and how Kristin has caused Trent's death.

It had taken six of us to split them up after that comment when Kristin went at Olivia in a rage I had never seen before or since. After that fight, Kristin had banished Olivia and told her that if she ever saw her again, she'd kill her on the spot.

I think the hardest part of all of that was watching Gabe leave with Olivia. All of us had liked Gabe, and he was like a brother to Kristin. After they left, it was months before she would even speak their names.

I blinked back to the present and watched Hugh leave, his bare ass glowing in the darkness near the door. "What an ass," I said softly, and my sister laughed. I winced, totally forgetting for a moment who was with me. "Sorry."

"Oh, no, don't be. He does have a nice ass," she replied. "What's up? You seem frustrated."

"Yeah, we have a little situation that needs your attention."

"What is it?"

"Um, I'm going to let Clayton and the board fill you in on that."

"I just talked to Clayton, and he didn't say anything."

"He just found out."

"Fine, let me change, and then I'll come down to the office." I followed my sister down the stairs. "Anything else happening around here?"

"Other than about a hundred calls congratulating you on your mating."

"Ugh, I'm glad I missed those. I did speak to Jacques Berger, and he wanted to know when we were going to have a celebration."

"It's not a bad idea. It would probably be smart for you and Hugh to make a public appearance pretty quickly."

"He doesn't want to until he speaks to work."

"He doesn't want to what?" Hugh asked as we hit the living room, and he was stepping out in slacks and a lavender button-down shirt. The shirt made his eyes brighter, and I looked away, irritated that I even noticed.

"We have received quite a few congratulations, and there has been some mention of a gathering to celebrate our mating."

A sexy smile slipped over his lips. "Really? You mean something like a wedding reception?"

I laughed at him. "More like a reason to drink, gorge ourselves on food, sex, and blood."

"Oh, more like an orgy." He laughed. "I like it."

I threw my head back and laughed. "You like that? I seem to remember when you were afraid of even being in the same room with Kristin and me; now you are thinking about having a vampire orgy."

"No, he's not," Kristin stated in an annoyed voice.

"That's not what he was saying upstairs," I said and then fought not to wince as Kristin glanced at Hugh and then me.

He shrugged. "What? She was watching, and I asked if she wanted to join."

"No, just no," Kristin said. "I share enough with her. I will not share my mate with her, at least the sex part."

Hugh put his arm around her and pulled her close. "Don't worry, Mistress. You are all I need." He kissed her once and then let her go.

"Let me get changed." She started to turn.

"You might want to bring Hugh with you to this meeting," I said, trying to hide my nervousness.

She popped a brow. "Does something they have to say have direct relations to him?"

"It could," I replied cryptically and blocked my mind so she couldn't dig around.

"Fine, I'll bring him with me." She disappeared into the bedroom without another word.

I rolled my eyes at Hugh as he turned to me. "All you need? You are very full of yourself, Mr. McMurphy."

"What? Just because I said she was all I needed, didn't mean that I didn't *want* other things."

"Be careful what you wish for, Hugh," I hissed quietly toward him. "Tell my sister that I will be down in the conference room."

"Will do," he stated, and I hightailed it out of the room. Being alone around Hugh right now was not a good idea.

I was happy for my sister, I was, and I looked forward to seeing what those two could accomplish together. Maybe we'd find out sooner rather than later. Once Kristin heard the news, she was going to blow a gasket.

I was in the conference room at the far end of the table when Kristin and Hugh joined the group looking refreshed and, weirdly, in love. The room was packed, and a few people—Rex, Cora, and Paxton—were especially tense.

Kristin let her gaze slip around the room, and it paused on Rex. Her eyes narrowed, and before she was seated, my sister had turned back into the intense and powerful vampire that she was. No more sweet and sexy with stars in her eyes, she now had her fangs ready to spring forward to shed blood.

"Give me the details."

Clayton spoke up. "I sent Joshua on an errand to retrieve some information for us about a hotspot in Baltimore where some of the breed was getting a little footloose and fancy-free. He was on his way back tonight as soon as the sun set when Cora felt his anxiety and anger, and then a brief spurt of pain from him. Since they are only bonded and not mated, she only captured the strongest of his feelings."

"This happened tonight? How long ago?"

Clayton glanced across the table at Beckett before he cleared his throat. "About an hour ago."

"Did you know about this when you came to see me?"

"Yes, but barely."

Her eyes shimmered in silver. "I'm only going to say this one more fucking time." She encompassed the entire group. "No one, and I mean no one is to keep anything of importance from me." She nailed Rex with a heated look. "If someone comes on this property, if someone disappears, if someone takes a shit and it could affect our way of life, I want to know about it immediately."

"I wanted to have more facts for you, Kristin, and you have been a little distracted." She glared at Clayton after he spoke.

"My priority is to my breed, not my hormones. Now, what the hell else do we know?" Kristin asked.

Jett answered. "We found his transport; it was in an abandoned lot in South Philly, but it was moved after the incident occurred."

"What do you mean, it was moved?"

Clayton stepped back into the conversation. "Cora came to me minutes after it happened, and we tracked his transport. It was moving, and then it stopped about ten minutes later. Jett was already heading that way since Cora couldn't reach him.

Paxton tried too, but neither could she. Joshua's transport was empty," he paused. "There was the scent of a human inside."

"A human?" Kristin raised a brow. "Are you telling me that a human captured Joshua?"

"We believe so," Clayton replied.

"And we know nothing else?"

"No," Clayton answered at the same time that Rex began to spout off.

"I know that humans just declared war!"

"Rex, that's enough. We will locate Josh." Kristin sat back in her chair, her eyes focused on the table, then she lifted them slowly to Hugh.

For a moment, the two of them looked at each other, and then Kristin abruptly turned away. "What are we doing?"

"The transport was towed back here, and we have feelers out, but so far nothing," Clayton stated.

"And now?"

"Now we have others out searching for information," Jett replied quickly.

"Alright, I do not want anyone to be out alone. In fact, not even in pairs. Right now, let's make sure that everyone who is outside of these walls has at least two other people with them at all times."

"Why three?" Jett asked.

"Because if they can get someone like Joshua that easily, they could probably get two people just as easily. Add in a third, and the chances are higher that at least one will get away."

"Or killed," Rex muttered.

"Yes, or killed, but even that could give us some hint as to what is going on." She stood. "I want updates every hour until he is found."

"What are you going to do now, Kristin?" Beckett asked as she stepped away from her desk.

"I'm going to do my own investigating. Hugh, Angelina,

Clayton, Ryker, and Conner, come with me, please. The rest of you reach out to every contact you have and get to work. I want Joshua found ASAP. I assume you all know just how important he is to me, and our breed, so find him!"

We all went down the hall and to Kristin's office. Once in, she looked at the door, and Ryker closed it as everyone got seated. Kristin wasn't even in her seat entirely when she nailed Hugh with a look that made me cringe.

"What the fuck is your task force up to?"

He stiffened. "Excuse me?"

"No, I will not. You and Singer came in here weeks ago and wanted a list of my people and a list of their abilities. I know for a fact that every single person who is missing has a unique ability. So what the hell is your task force doing?"

"Kristin, they aren't doing anything," he stated, looking slightly shell-shocked at her tone.

"The hell they aren't. I told you about Josh! About what his ability was, and now he goes missing! That is not a coincidence, Agent McMurphy!" she snapped. "If I'm not mistaken, I told you that in confidence. I did not tell you that so that you could take it back to your water cooler and share with your boys."

A muscle ticked in his jaw. "I did not tell anyone, Mistress," he growled back at her, his eyes getting a little brighter. Oh, wow! "I swear to you that I did not tell anyone about Josh or what he can do. I told you that I would not tell them anything unless you said it was alright. I have never broken that confidence."

Along with everyone else in the room, we watched the two of them, knowing they were speaking confidentially. Finally, Kristin sighed and rubbed her temples for a moment as she put her elbows on her desk.

"Is it possible that your government is using that list that you are trying to create for their own purposes?"

"Of course, it's possible. A lot of people have access to it, and

I can bet some of them want to use your abilities with some of our military forces."

"Do you agree with that?" she asked him point-blank.

"I do not, and that has nothing to do with what is going on in my personal life now. I never felt that way."

Kristin sat back in her seat, twisting left and right for a few moments as her mind worked the problem. After a few moments of silence, Clayton spoke up.

"Hugh, do you have anyone that you can ask? Anyone that you know that would trust you enough to tell you maybe something was going on behind the scenes?"

He rubbed his jaw. "Maybe. I could try to speak with Steve Winwood. He's my direct supervisor outside of the task force."

"Alright, do you have any idea where he lives?" Clayton asked.

"I do."

"Then I think maybe you need to visit."

Hugh turned to my sister, and she nodded her consent. "Yeah, that might be a good idea. Ryker and Conner will go with you for safety, and I want Cameron to go too."

"He might think it is odd that I am showing up with a bunch of men."

I laughed. "So what? Do you not remember that you just mated with the Mistress? You are now high up on everyone's list to acquire. Get used to the bodyguards, Hugh."

"Angelina is right," Clayton stated. "You are now a coveted prize to be collected. You might also consider telling your boss which side you are now on, and that life has changed for you."

"I thought I would have time before I had to do that," Hugh stated.

"Why do you need time, Hugh?" Kristin asked. "You are one of us now, and you can't go back. You won't be able to work daylight hours with them; you sure as hell can't share with them what you know. The day you mated with me is the day you declared your allegiance to me and our breed."

He looked pissed, but he rolled his shoulders back after a moment and spoke. "Will I be able to work with them at all? Be a liaison as we previously spoke about?"

Kristin's eyes lightened to a light gray. "Well, that is going to depend on if they were responsible for kidnapping my man. If they did, there would never be a liaison; there would only be a war that they declared upon themselves."

CHAPTER NINETEEN

KRISTIN

*W*hen I saw in Rex's mind that Joshua was missing, my anger threatened to erupt. I wasn't sure how I kept as calm as I did because I instantaneously wanted to pitch people from the windows, crush things with my bare hands, roar until the building collapsed around me, and then find blood to spill.

As they all talked, my mind kept going back to Hugh. I watched him, waiting for anything that would tell me he knew about this. But his expression and thoughts only showed concern for me. Did Portage have something to do with this? Or was this the work of that fucking task force?

"Do you know anything about this?" I asked him silently, careful to keep my tone calm.

"No, of course not. Why would I know anything?"

"I needed to ask."

"Why would you think I knew anything about this?" I didn't respond. *"Are you okay, Kris?"*

"I'm fine," I stated and locked down my mind again.

When we headed into my office, I was fit to be tied. Something was going on, and I didn't like it. It had to be humans; this was not the work of my enemy. How dare mere humans take Joshua—or any of my people. What was their ultimate agenda? Were they building an army for themselves—or trying to get to me?

I had words with Hugh again, trying hard to focus on his mind as I questioned him. At no time did he appear to be hiding anything from me, and I had to accept that he was telling me the truth and didn't know anything about them taking members of our breed.

"Lena, tell Cameron to come here."

"On it," she replied as everyone got up to leave.

"Ryker, Conner, hold on a second," I said out loud to them.

Silently, I spoke with my sister. *"Get Hugh out of here for a few minutes and keep him busy."*

She didn't even reply to me, just went right up to Hugh and snaked her arm around his. "Come on, big boy. Let's go get a snack before we all head out and find Kristin's boy toy."

"Boy toy?" Hugh asked with a chuckle and glanced back at me as I rolled my eyes.

With only Ryker and Conner in the room now, I motioned for them to sit. "Look, guys, I need you all to be on extra alert."

"Are you worried about someone coming after Hugh?" Conner asked.

The door opened, and I waved Cameron in. "Have a seat, Cam." I turned my attention back to Conner. "I am concerned that he could become a target, but I need you guys zeroed in on him. I am about to read you all in on something that does not leave this room. Do you understand?"

They all acknowledged with a nod. "When I mated with Hugh, there was something in his memories that was essentially closed off. I'm not sure exactly what it was, but I only got a glimpse of it before it was gone. Hugh's mind generally seems very open, but he has a blind spot in there. Even Clayton noticed it but didn't think much of it during the transition."

"Has he been compelled?" Ryker asked.

"That's what I'm thinking, but I don't know what he was compelled to do." There was no reason to tell them what I did know—not now. Letting them know that they needed to keep a close eye on him was enough. Of course, I was pretty sure he had been compelled to find me, but what else?

Cam seemed concerned. "Have you spoken to him about it?"

"No, and neither will any of you. Ryker and Conner will continue to be his guards, but Cam, I need you to be there too and measure his mind. See if you can see past the compulsion. Look for any signs of it or any signs that his human boss has been compelled."

"Alright, I can do that."

"Plus, it would be good to have a seasoned agent on this one to help him. Guide him through how we do things. He needs his eyes open to our world—and fast."

"Of course," Cameron said at once with a sly grin. "I love nothing more than breaking in the newbies."

Ryker cleared his throat. "Mistress, I don't mean to overstep my bounds, but if he's been compromised, do you think it is safe to remain mated to him? Shouldn't you possibly break that bond—at least for now—until we know more?"

"Ryker, I appreciate your concern and your willingness to speak out on that concern, I sincerely do. I have thought it over long and hard. I have no reason to believe that Hugh is a threat to me. He could have been compelled to forget a random secret or a location; we don't know. We need to be vigilant and listen in on his mind, watch what he does, measure the truth in his words." I paused. "I need all three of you to remain close to him and not only protect him but protect me from him if there is an ulterior motive."

"Do you think there is?" Conner asked.

I smirked his way. "I'm pretty sure there is an ulterior motive for just about anything in our world."

Cameron laughed and then winked at me as if that told him that there was way more to this story than I was letting on. He could believe what he wanted.

"Gentleman, before you go." I lifted my hand, felt my eyes change, and the familiar hum in my blood. "You will not repeat this information to anyone. You will only speak of it with me behind closed doors, and when we are alone."

I let my hand drop down, and they all blinked. "Yes, Mistress," Ryker said. Cameron and Conner both said yes too, and then I told Ryker to fill Cameron in on their task as they left to find Hugh.

I sat back in my chair after they left and reached out for Joshua. I felt nothing, but then I was pretty sure I wouldn't feel anything either. These people knew what they were doing, and they knew how to mask our powers. Once they grabbed Joshua, he was probably moved instantly to a truck lined with platinum and titanium so that Joshua would feel weak and couldn't communicate with us.

For a moment, I wondered why I wasn't more upset now, but then I realized that these people were keeping Joshua safe for a specific reason. Probably not to get to me, although they might be trying to obtain information about me and the breed. But if the humans took him, they wanted him for a purpose, and because of that, I knew he was safe—for now.

We would find him. I would move heaven and earth to locate him again. God help the people who took him and the rest of the people involved or the ones that got in my way to find him. I pushed a button on my phone. "Lainey, get me all the information that we have on the missing people and see if Mick is around to help me."

"Yes, Mistress."

Mick was my old police partner, and from time to time, I'd call him in and get his opinion on some things. Several missing people was something that the two of us could look into together. Maybe we'd find some other details that others had missed before. It was worth a try.

Almost thirty minutes later, Mick walked in with a tablet in his hands. "Lainey said she put everything on this." He set it on the desk and took a seat. "How's married life treating you?"

I chuckled. "I'm not married, Mick, and you know that."

"It's just like being married—almost. How are things? He seems like a nice guy; I guess you noticed his eyes look a lot like Julian's did." I winced. Mick always said the first thing that came to his mind.

Once in a while, I would gaze into Hugh's eyes and be struck by how similar to Julian's they were. That was the only similarity, though, the color of his eyes. He was taller than Julian. He stood differently, with his head up, ready to come at you head-on. Julian had looked at you more from under his lashes; he was quieter, more intense—more animalistic.

Ugh, I did not need to be thinking about Julian. I shoved thoughts of him to the side as Mick pushed a few buttons on the tablet, and a computer text popped up in front of us. "Make that bigger so we can read it easier."

He did, and then we sat back. "What are we looking for?"

"Anything that will lead us to Joshua."

He was quiet for a moment, and I realized he was watching me. "We'll find him."

"Of that, I have no doubt, Mick."

"Who do you think took him? Tell me what your thoughts are so I can keep them in mind as we go through all this."

"I believe there are two possible options here. Either Joseph Portage took him, or the task force that Hugh oversaw is involved."

"Why would they take him?"

"When I first met Hugh, he was asking for a list of our breed and wanted to know who had abilities and what they were. I refused to tell him, but that didn't stop me wondering why they wanted them. Not long ago, I mentioned in a personal conversation with Hugh that Joshua could hide me, and now he is missing."

"You think Hugh told them?"

"I don't know. He could have, or there could be other people involved who have found the information and used it. It's not like we have hidden the knowledge that he can do that very well."

"So, you told Hugh about Josh?"

"I did."

"You sure he's not involved?"

"Yes." I turned to Mick. The more I thought about it, the more sure I was. "I am convinced that Hugh has nothing to do with Josh being taken. Right now, Hugh, Cameron, Ryker, and Conner are heading to Hugh's boss' house to find out what he knows. If he knows anything."

"You think he won't?"

"It's a possibility. This whole thing might go a lot higher up than Hugh's supervisor."

"You seem to be leaning heavily on the task force or government having something to do with this, and not Portage."

I pursed my lips. "This isn't his style. He's very in your face. If this had been Portage, he would have taken Joshua more dramatically. What would his reason be anyway?"

"To use Josh against you. If he knew that Josh could hide you, which I'm sure he does—like you said, it's not a well-kept secret. He could force Josh to hide him. Maybe he wants to come after you."

"That is a possibility, but I don't think the probability is very high on that."

Mick shrugged. "Stranger things have happened."

"That is true."

For a moment, I focused on the computer screen in front of us, but I felt Mick shifting back and forth on something. It immediately flashed me back to a point in time after I'd first transitioned, and Mick had just learned what I was. I could always feel when he wanted to ask me about something.

I sighed. "What's on your mind, Mick?"

"How many reborns do you think are out there?"

My eyes opened wide in surprise. "Where the hell did that question come from?"

He turned to me, his dark-brown eyes searching mine. "I just thought if you found Hugh and he's like three times removed, how many others are out there?"

"I don't know, Mick, but between you and me, I want to find out."

It was his turn to look surprised. "Are you serious?"

"Yes, in fact, I'm already working on something."

"You are?"

I nodded. "Yes, but please keep that between us."

"Absolutely! Is there anything I can do to help?"

I smiled at him. "Maybe. I'll let you know if there is."

"Wouldn't it be awesome if you found out Julian was still alive?"

I froze for a second, my voice coming out much softer than I would have hoped for. "Why would you even say that, Mick?"

He turned. "Sorry, Kris, I didn't mean to upset you, but what if? I know you saw him fall over the cliff, but you said his body was never recovered. He might not have been turned to ash when he fell. He could have been eaten by animals or burned in the sun. What if his heart wasn't punctured?"

The scene flashed through my mind, and I thought I would vomit. Adam and Julian had been on a mountain pass in Colorado, looking for a breed member who was stalking and raping women as they hiked and camped in the area. I had recently come out to visit with Julian and check in on things in the Western VMF office. Julian had invited me to join them on this mission, much to Adam's displeasure. I'd never been a fan of Adam's, but Julian said he was an excellent agent.

While searching, we had split up at one point, and I was exploring in a separate area. I'd felt anguish flash through my bond with Julian, and it almost took me to my knees. I could think of only one thing that would cause that kind of feeling—the loss of a mate. I had felt it myself just a year earlier with Trent.

I'd rushed back to comfort Julian, but instead, I'd found Julian and Adam in a vicious battle. I don't know if I distracted Julian, or if something else did, because Adam suddenly got the upper hand, and in one quick movement, he sliced Julian's throat. My eyes had locked with Julian's, and I knew that this was what he had seen forty years ago when I—my old self, as Calista—had been murdered by Damon—Julian's son.

I screamed as panic and realization filled his gaze, and Adam shoved him back over the cliff edge. I felt my life bond with Julian snap just two seconds later, and it almost felt worse than losing Trent. Suddenly my chest was eerily hollow—empty—alone.

Adam had spun on me, surprised that I was there, and before I could even think to attack him, he turned and fled. I knew I would see Adam again one day and exact my vengeance, so instead, I searched for a way to get down the cliff without killing myself and eventually got down to the bottom. It didn't take me long to find Julian's broken body.

For a few moments, I had stood frozen a few feet away, and then I had fallen to my knees and cried as I had never cried before.

Adam had torn open his throat and then thrown him about two hundred feet down into the ravine. Julian must have bounced down the slope because bones were snapped and exposed, and his beautiful face was battered, bruised, and misshapen. My hands fluttered over his body, unsure what to do

—but there was nothing that I could do. No amount of blood would fix him—not now.

When I finally got control over myself, I knelt beside him, a stake raised high in my hand as I prepared to send him back to our maker, but then I paused. I had always told Julian that this hadn't been our time, but what if he returned? What if when he did, it was our time? Could I possibly live in a world where Julian didn't exist?

I could if I thought that he might one day return to me.

I put the stake back into my pocket and looked around. It had taken me too long to get down here, and the sun would be rising soon. There was no way I would be able to get us both back to safety before the sun rose. While I could take some sun, I would not be able to handle it for long—not long enough to get us back to where our vehicle should have been. I had little doubt that it would still be there—no thanks to Adam.

I was going to need to find someplace to shelter for the day. I stared at his broken body and realized that I couldn't take him back like this anyway—no one needed to see this. If Lyssa was alive, she did not need to see this, and Lorna didn't need this image to haunt her young mind.

Instead, I lifted Julian and carried him into a clearing. I laid his body to rest in the field near an outcropping of rocks. The sun was just starting to lighten the eastern sky as I removed his shirt and folded it neatly. The more skin visible, the faster he would burn.

Oh, my god! I was going to put Julian into the sun. My heart knotted in my chest as my stomach filled with acid. I would never look into his beautiful eyes, never hear his voice again. I hunched over him, crying for every moment of our life and how there would never be another one.

Tears ran unchecked down my cheeks as those moments, good and bad, raced through my mind. As the first rays of sun began to crest the horizon, I leaned forward and kissed his scarred forehead one last time.

"Return to me, Julian. Return to me, and we will finally have our time. Find me, please. I'll be waiting for you, Jules." I caressed his cheek. "I will always love you, Julian. Find me."

A ray of sun struck my face, and I shielded it as I took one last look at Julian and then raced back into the trees. I stood in the deep shadow of a copse of trees, waiting for Julian's body to go up in flames. It didn't take long, and the moisture continued to roll down my cheeks until he was nothing but smoldering ash.

Find me, Julian, find me! I had prayed to whoever could hear me, and then I had spent the next couple of daylight hours going from one darkened area to another, finally finding a small cave that blocked the worst of the sunrays. I had collapsed there and cried myself to sleep.

When I woke, I returned to where I had laid Julian, and I collected his pocket knife, watch face, and stakes, and then I walked away to wait for him to return.

It had been thirty-five years, and I had not found him—or he had not found me. Was Jules out there someplace living as a human male? Had he transitioned? Did he know who I was? Did memories of me ever come to him?

I tried to smile at Mick. "You never know, do you? Like you said earlier, stranger things have happened."

CHAPTER TWENTY

HUGH

I was rather fascinated by the woman I had mated. I knew she was close to Josh, knew that he was essential to her, and I had expected her to lose her shit—but she didn't. Agents in my office had turned into raving lunatics at much less.

Yes, she was rightfully angry, but her ability to remain calm, cool, and collected amazed me. The only telltale sign that she was upset most of the time was her changing eyes. Sometimes they morphed so rapidly from one color to another that it was like someone had flipped a switch. They astonished me—utterly amazed me.

I understood why Kristin was asking me if the task force was involved. I got it, although I didn't particularly appreciate being accused of something I wasn't involved with. But I understood it and her need to question me.

What pissed me off more was Kristin telling me that I had made my decision when I had mated with her. Essentially, I had, and I knew that, but I wasn't a fan of how she threw that in my face. Maybe part of me thought that I could pretend and keep a piece of my old life, but as I stood around and observed the tense manner of everyone in the room, I knew that had been a fantasy.

I just hoped that my task force wasn't involved with this because I had never signed on for something like that. That had nothing to do with the fact that I was a vampire now. I wouldn't have agreed with it as a human, either.

Angelina and I took the elevator, and I turned to her. "Do your eyes change color as drastically as hers do?"

She shook her head. "No, mine turn icy white when I am pissed or intense, but they don't change color with my every emotion."

"Can she control that?"

"If she's paying attention. When she is around humans or others where she needs to be more guarded, she will, but it was good for all of them to see her royally pissed off. It keeps them on their toes. If I know my sister, and I do, then she is ready to shed some blood."

"Would she?"

Angelina stared up at me. "What? Shed blood? In a heartbeat to protect one of our own."

"Can she fight?"

Angelina laughed. "She is fierce, Hugh. Don't even doubt that. She might appear to sit on a throne, but that woman could take your head off before you could blink, and she could do it with her bare hands."

"Good to know. I'll try not to piss Kris off."

"Smart idea," Angelina commented quietly.

"Have you ever pissed her off?" I asked, and she started to snicker.

"Oh, there was a time when she wanted to skin me alive, and quite a few times since that she hasn't been quite so happy with me, but for the most part, we work well together. I know how to calm her when she is ready to snap, and she knows that I am willing to do anything for her."

"Would you?"

"Would I what?"

"Do anything for her?"

"Absolutely."

"So, if Kristin told you to kill someone, you'd do it?"

Angelina pursed her lips and shook her head. "I think we already determined that killing someone is not an issue for me, Hugh."

"But would you do it without knowing why? Just because she told you to do it?"

The elevator door opened, and I followed her out. She stopped a few feet from the door. "If my sister told me to jump, I'd ask her how high and off what building. If she told me to give someone a buzz cut, I'd ask her if she wanted it done with scissors or a razor. If she told me to have sex with you, I'd ask her how many times should I make you orgasm and what position she wanted me to be in. If she asked me to take someone's life, I'd ask her how long I had to complete the job, and in what method. It does not matter the why of it; if she asked, then I'd consider it a command. She is my Mistress; I obey her."

Angelina turned and looked around, waving her hand. "You would be hard-pressed to find anyone around here that wouldn't do the same thing. You need to ask yourself, Hugh, if you are willing to follow her without question."

"That's not something that I have ever done before. What makes these people do it so willingly?"

"Because they believe in her. They trust that she knows what she is doing and that she has their best interests in mind."

"And they all believe that?"

"Those that don't are with Portage. With the research you have done on our breed, what did you learn? Are there more that follow her or him?"

"Without a doubt, her."

"Just like any government, Hugh, there will always be people who don't agree with something, but you have to believe in the bigger picture."

"Alright, I get that."

"Then you better decide, and quickly, if you are going to get on the bandwagon because I'm pretty sure that she doesn't have the time or patience to deal with you being wishy-washy. You are either with her—and the breed—or you aren't."

"Okay, I get it, Angelina. I guess part of me thought that I could still keep a foot in my old world."

"Not even a sexy little toe."

I chuckled. "You think my toes are sexy?"

She rolled her eyes. "You're missing the point, and I have no clue about your toes. I have never paid attention to your feet; now your ass"—she stepped around me—"that I know is sexy."

I caught up to her. "You'd really have sex with me if she told you to?"

"In your dreams," she muttered, but I saw the touch of a smile on her pouty mouth.

I laughed heartily as I accompanied her into the lounge where we took a seat and ordered something to eat. A few minutes later, Ryker, Conner, and Cameron joined us, and we finished our meal with them, and then I said goodbye to Angelina.

Cameron and Conner sat in front of the transport and were quiet on the way to my boss' house. I sat in the back with Ryker, and we bullshitted about sports for a while in between me giving Conner directions. I knew how to get there, but I had no clue what his address was.

When we pulled up out front, I reached for the button to open the door. "You know this might go over much better if it's just me," I said.

"Ryker and Conner can stay out here near the car, but I'm going in with you," Cameron stated as he looked back over the seat.

"Okay."

Cameron matched my stride on the way to the front door. I could feel Ryker and Conner behind us, and I was a little amazed at how intense they were now that they were outside of the transport.

"Let me know if you need anything," Ryker said softly into my head.

"I will," I responded, thinking it was weird to have that big guy's voice whispering into my mind. Cameron chuckled next to me, and I gave him an odd look. He just shook his head at me and let me ring the doorbell.

We could all hear the footsteps in the house, the sound of water running, a woman's voice asking who could be here this late. It all seemed surreal. A few days ago, I wouldn't have been able to hear those things. The front porch light flipped on, and I turned so that Steve could see my face in his camera screen on the other side.

The door opened without delay. "Hugh, what are you doing here? Is there a problem?" His gaze cut from me and hit Cameron before looking past us at Ryker and Conner. His brows furrowed. "What's going on?"

"Hey, Steve, sorry for showing up like this, but I need to speak with you about a critical matter."

"Who are these people?"

I glanced back at Ryker and Conner, their faces stoic and almost downright scary. "Don't worry about those guys; bodyguards for my friend here." I poked a thumb at Cameron.

"Hi, Steve, I'm Cameron Fields." Cam held his hand out to Steve, and he shook it and relaxed immediately. Oddly, I felt him relax, and I found that rather interesting. How was I able to feel that?

As we stepped into the house, Cameron spoke into my mind. *"Most of us can feel surges of emotions; only some can feel the tiny shifts."*

"Good to know."

"Can I offer you a drink?" Steve looked between the two of us.

"Sure, I'd love whatever you are having," Cameron responded, and I echoed that. Steve brought us into his office and closed the door after telling his wife he'd be a few minutes.

"So, what is so important that you needed to come here tonight and speak with me?" He paused. "I thought you were on leave for your health?"

"Yes, I am on leave, but this couldn't wait," I replied.

I glanced at Cameron, but he was smiling as he lifted his glass to his lips. *"Start by asking him about the task force and the reason for the ability list."*

"I think I know what I'm doing here, Cameron; I've been in law enforcement for a long time. But thanks for the heads-up," I replied back and then directed my next words to my boss. "Steve, I need you to be frank with me."

He frowned. "Haven't I always been, Hugh?"

"I'd like to think that you have, but something isn't adding up right now, and I need to understand why."

"What's that?"

"Why are we asking for a list of vampire abilities? I mean, as we catalog people in and find them, we are compiling a list of what they can do. Why are we doing that?"

Steve laughed as he glanced between Cameron and me. "Why do we create a list of anything? So we can track it, Hugh. Why are you asking about this?"

"Are you aware of any agency using that list to its advantage?"

Steve shifted in his seat slightly. "Hugh, why are you asking about this?"

"Steve, I'm aware that many of the vampires that are on that list have recently gone missing."

"Missing?" His forehead lined. "What are you talking about, Hugh? How do you even know that?"

"Are we kidnapping vampires and holding them someplace? And if we are, why?"

"What?" He laughed. "Why would we do that?"

"Why? Because these missing vampires are special; they can do some off-the-wall things. I could see why our government might want to use them. I just need to know if they are."

"No, I am not aware of them doing any of that."

"You're not?"

I glanced at Cameron. *"Is he being truthful or lying?"*

"Truthful, but he's hiding something."

"Do you know anything about this, Steve?"

Steve focused on Cameron. "Who exactly are you?"

Cameron smiled again. "Cameron Fields."

"And why are you here with Hugh? What is your interest in this?"

"My interest is that I believe *your* government is taking *my* people and locking them up someplace to use them."

I felt Steve's fear begin to rise as he sank back into his chair. "You're a vampire? Those men outside protecting you, they are vampires too?"

"Yes, I am, and they are, but they aren't protecting me; they are protecting Hugh. We are not going to hurt you, Steve. At least, we don't want to. What we want to know is who is taking our breed members."

He shook his head, looking uncomfortable. "I don't know. I don't even know for sure that they are. I will admit that I did overhear something relevant to this, but I don't know any of the details."

"Is there someone that you can ask?" I stepped back into the conversation.

"Hugh," he paused and peered at Cameron closely, "please do not take offense to this, Mr. Fields, but I can't believe you brought one of them here to confront me like this. My family is here, damn it! Why are they protecting you?"

"Relax, Steve, your family is safe. We aren't going to do anything to them," Cameron stated.

"We?" Steve looked back and forth at us. "Are you including Hugh in on that?"

"Yes, I am. You already mentioned that you were aware that Hugh took a leave of absence," Cameron stated.

"Cam, I got this," I interrupted him before he could go on. He didn't have any right to tell my boss what was going on in my life.

"Hugh, what the hell is going on?" Steve demanded.

"Steve, I recently found out something about myself. It explains why I had such an interest in vampire affairs. Come to find out, I am one of them."

Steve's face blanched. "What?"

"I'm a vampire, Steve. I took time off to figure out what to do, and I decided to transition and join the lifestyle."

"Join the lifestyle? What the hell does that mean?" I could feel not only his fear but his confusion.

"It means that I'm a vampire now, Steve."

"How can you be a vampire? How could you not know you were? This makes no sense, Hugh! Did they somehow create you? Are you one of those humans turned into a vampire?"

"No, I am not a human-turned."

"*Show him your teeth,*" Cameron said.

"*No!*"

"*Oh, come on, it's the easiest way to prove to someone that you are telling the truth. Just flash your fangs, and we can get out of here. This guy doesn't know anything of value—yet.*"

I sighed mentally. "Steve, it's kind of complicated, but I found out that my great-grandfather was a vampire, and I carried the gene."

He laughed louder. "I don't believe this shit—carried a gene? What the fuck is that?"

Cameron chuckled, and I sighed loudly and closed my eyes. A moment later, I convinced my teeth to come out, and I opened my mouth enough for him to see them.

"Holy shit!" he said as fear ripped through his system, and he grabbed the arm of his chair, the highball glass in his other hand almost tipping to the side.

"Relax, Steve. I'm not going to hurt you."

Before Steve could say anything further, Cameron flashed to the other side of the room and held Steve's neck at an odd angle to expose his neck.

"What the fuck are you doing?" I hissed.

"Come here and feed from him."

"No! Are you nuts!"

Cameron glared at me. *"It's time to learn our ways—your ways. Get over here and drink from him so you can compel him. Now get over here before he screams and brings the family in. Just relax. I know what I'm doing."*

Fear flooded the room as I got to my feet, and Steve's gaze jumped to the door and then back to me. Fear for his family is what kept him from screaming—somehow, I just knew this.

"Don't do this, Hugh," Steve begged.

I glanced at Cameron. "How much do I need to take?"

"A couple of mouthfuls," he returned. "Just do it, quick."

I closed my eyes for a moment, allowed my fangs to come back down, and then I could suddenly smell his human blood as if it was all that surrounded me. My mouth watered for something that I didn't understand, and I snapped down on his neck. A moment later, Steve moaned, and Cameron put his hand over his mouth to muffle the sound.

The blood was terrific, although very different than Kristin's sweet essence. I filled my mouth and swallowed three times before I released him and licked the puncture marks.

171

"Now what?"

"Now, get him to face you and focus on him, like you are looking right into his brain, and tell him what you want him to do."

"You make it sound easy."

Cameron grinned. *"I think for you, it will be."*

I spun the chair until Steve faced me, his skin pale, a sheen of sweat over his brow. I leaned down into his face, focusing on his eyes. "Steve, you are going to help us. You are going to see what you can find out about who is taking the vampires, and then you are going to call me. When you snap out of this, you aren't going to be afraid of me, and while you will be aware of my new secret, you will not be able to tell anyone. Do you understand?"

Steve nodded. "Yes, I understand."

"Perfect," Cameron said as he let go of Steve's head. He returned to his chair and took a seat as if nothing had happened and nodded to me to do the same thing.

Once I was seated, Cameron snapped his fingers, and Steve startled like he'd been staring off in space. He frowned to himself and turned his chair back to us.

Cameron stood. "Well, if you remember anything, you know who to call. Thank you for the drink, Steve." He smiled at him, baring his fangs as he did so, and Steve turned even paler—if that were possible.

"Steve, give me a call if you think of anything. I'll be in touch." I stood and nodded to my boss, who wasn't sure what he should do. "We will show ourselves out."

After we got outside, Cameron spoke softly. "He doesn't know, but there is more to the story. I do not doubt that he will start making some calls now."

"Did I compel him in there?"

"You did, and you did amazingly for your first time." He slapped me on the back. "You're a natural, just like your mate."

"What do we do now?"

"We wait."

After we all piled back inside the transport, Cameron turned to look back at me. "So, what did you think of that?"

I started to laugh. "If I admit that I liked that, is that a problem?"

Conner and Ryker began to laugh, and Cameron grinned. "No, the problem would be if you didn't like it. It only gets more fun from here."

CHAPTER TWENTY-ONE

JOSHUA

*W*as it wrong to wish death on her new mate? Probably. Did I care? Not one fucking bit. Was I a douche for that? Probably. Should I respect her decision and support her? Absolutely. Was I going to? Not on this one, I wasn't.

From the moment the guy arrived, I had been on edge with him. Yeah, he seemed like he was a nice enough guy, but I didn't trust him. How can you not know what you are? And how the fuck could he work with a task force that was trying to destroy us?

I climbed into the elevator and watched Kristin disappear into her apartment. I still had no idea why she came to me earlier and demanded that I think of Alex's death, and it made me seriously wonder. Had she seen something in his mind about it? That was impossible. The guy would have been in his early twenties, and if he had been there, I would have remembered him.

So what was it? What did he possibly know about that day? It was just another fucking reason not to like the guy. Not that I needed one.

I went down to the offices and found Clayton in his. "Mistress told me to check in with you since she's otherwise busy."

Clayton raised his head from what he was reading. "Bitter much?"

"The guy is a douche."

"The guy is her mate and could one day be your master, so I'd watch your mouth, Joshua."

I laughed as I took a seat. "There is no fucking way I would ever follow that guy—never."

Clayton set his tablet on his desk and stared at me. "I suggest that you think long and hard about that comment, Joshua. You could very easily find yourself tossed out on your ass."

"She wouldn't do that."

He laughed. "I didn't think she would ever get rid of her best friend, but she kicked her ass to the curb. Don't think she won't ban you if you piss her off enough. God knows you've been pushing the limit recently."

"What does that mean?"

"That stunt with taking her blood. That was stupid, reckless. You are important to her, Josh—to all of us. You keep pulling stunts like that, and it's going to get you killed or banned."

I shook my head. "I don't think so. She wouldn't do that."

He laughed. "You want to keep trying, be my guest, but I'm pretty sure your petty jealousy is the last thing on her mind."

"Whatever," I muttered. "She told me to see you, see if you have anything that you need accomplished."

"I do."

"Alright, tell me what it is so that I can get it over with."

"I need you to head down to Baltimore. There is a crew working the waterfront there that needs to be investigated. We got word on this about three days ago, but all the other agents that I would trust to oversee this are tied up right now."

"What are they doing in Baltimore?"

"Word has it that they have some odd human trafficking ring

going on in the process. Using the water to move people from one state to the other to hide them better."

"What do you want me to do?"

"I want confirmation that it is happening. I want to make sure they are moving humans and not our breed. Once we know for sure what is happening, then we can move forward with getting a team together to stop it. You'll be able to get in there without them knowing, and get back out."

"Alright, when do you want me to go?"

"Tonight. You should be able to start at least looking around if you leave soon. Give yourself a day to see what you learn and then get back to us the next night."

"You want me gone for two nights? What if Kris needs me?"

"Josh." He shook his head. "Kristin isn't going anywhere. I have no doubt that she will be locked in her apartment for the next couple of days."

Well, didn't that just piss in my beer? Actually, this was an excellent idea to get me the hell out of here for a few days. Then I wouldn't have to be around to feel it happening. "Let me grab some things, and then I'm outta here."

"Keep me updated," Clayton said as I slipped out of his office.

I went back to my apartment, and damn if I didn't feel the unleashed raw power of Kristin and her mate as they came together—again! I grabbed what I needed and couldn't wait to get the hell out of the building.

I was heading into the garage when I ran into Rex, and he asked, "Where are you going?"

"Running down to Baltimore to check things out for Clayton."

"I heard about that stuff down there. You going alone?"

"Yeah."

"I'm surprised he's sending you down. What about the mistress?"

I laughed; he hated referring to Kristin as his mother. "Your mom is busy." I stepped around him. "Hey, maybe you'll get a brother or sister out of the deal."

As soon as I said it, I wished that I hadn't. The last thing I wanted was to see those two get any closer. A child could forge a stronger bond with them.

"Watch it!" he shouted at me, but he was laughing. "The last thing my mom needs is another brat that I have to compete with!"

"True. See you when I get back."

"Yep, later." Rex waved, and he was gone.

THE TRIP WAS RELATIVELY easy and boring. I arrived in Baltimore, found out what I needed within a couple of hours, and could have headed back. I didn't. Instead, I found a cozy dive bar and a couple of women to occupy my time with and then decided to enjoy the two days away from work just to unwind and enjoy myself. How long was it since I had done that? Thirty years?

I was on my way back to Philly while I was wondering if I was about due. Maybe I should take a more extended vacation, hide in the mountains someplace for a couple of weeks. Maybe Cora or Paxton would want to get away—perhaps both of them would. Wonder if Rex could get away, too? We could ask Novah to come—Nah. I wasn't a fan of her, and Rex didn't seem all that into her either.

I was just hitting Philly when an electrical charge came out of nowhere and zapped the hell out of my transport. It was like a bolt of lightning had crashed from the sky directly into my transport. It died in the middle of the road, along with a bunch of other transports. What the fuck was that?

Doors opened on the other transports, and the occupants started to converge on me. Only they weren't just Tom, Dick,

Harry, and Jane. These people looked fucking military. The chopper that hovered over one of the transports off to the side confirmed it.

What the fuck! Before I could even kick myself into fight or flight mode, someone pointed something at me and fired. Another bolt of electricity slammed into me, practically frying my brain matter, and then the doors were ripped open on my transport and I was hauled out. A hood was pulled over my head, and a needle pressed into my arm. I tried to fight, but I felt my knees start to give, and then everything went black.

* * *

IT WAS like a switch had been flipped in my head, and I sprang upright, falling off the metal cot I'd been lying on. I was on my feet, spinning in a circle as I took in my surroundings. My head felt foggy, my limbs heavy as I finished my loop and stopped at a window.

I shuffled to the three-foot by four-foot window. In the glass was a metal wire, most likely titanium and platinum. That didn't bother me as much as what was on the other side. As I came to the window, I looked as far as I could see, one way, then the other, and found identical cells like mine.

Half of the cells that I could see were occupied, or I assumed they were filled as lights were on inside of them. A couple of the occupants stood at their window, staring out. Where the fuck was I?

I turned and looked at the eight-by-ten cell behind me with only a toilet, sink, and cot, and I felt the panic starting to claw it's way up my throat. What was this place? Are these all our missing people? Who the fuck was collecting us and putting us into specimen cages?

I turned back to the window and made eye contact with a man on the opposite side. His name was Charlie Zorin. I didn't personally know him, but I had seen his missing report. He was substantially stronger than most of us—like lift a fucking car over his head strong—and if he was still inside this place, then there was no chance in hell that I could break out.

Why did I have to be such a jealous prick? If I had just gone with the flow, I would have been back at the hotel, safe, sound, and able to protect Kristin.

My hands went to my head as I raked my fingers over my skull. "Fuck!"

CHAPTER TWENTY-TWO

JOSPEH

"What the hell do you mean, she's missing?" I growled at Adam. "Where did she go?"

"I don't know, Master." Adam swallowed nervously. "She was with us last night and went home, but she's gone, and no one can reach her now."

"Did someone go to her house?"

"Yeah, her mate said she never came home. He figured she was still working and crashed someplace because it got late."

I let my moody gaze drift around the room. "Could she be working someplace?"

"I mean, she could be, but I don't think so. She could be with Olivia too; she's missing also."

"Who is Olivia?"

"She's another human-turned who is mated to Gabe."

"What does she do?"

He grinned. "She's a wise-ass, but she's an air mover."

"Does Gabe know where she might have gone?"

He shook his head. "No, when we asked Gabe, he didn't know where Olivia was; he said that the last he had felt her was last night. He said while he can't feel her now, he doesn't think she's dead; she's just not there. If that makes sense."

I stood and went to get a drink. I poured two fingers of whiskey, threw it back, and then poured two more. "How can someone just not be there?"

Adam shrugged. "Maybe she's in the same place that the other missing people are."

I frowned. "How many are missing now?"

Adam shrugged again. "I think thirty-two, but I could be wrong."

"Thirty-two? Why the hell didn't anyone tell me this? When did everyone start disappearing?"

Adam shuffled his feet. "About a month ago, I guess. I didn't say anything because I was attempting to find them. I thought maybe they were trying to go off on their own and start a new rebellion."

I stared at him for a moment; was he a complete idiot? "We are talking about the same people, right? The ones that have decided to follow me, correct?"

"Well, um, yeah."

"Then I doubt very much that they have taken off on their own to start a new rebellion. I control them, Adam; they can't just go off on their own. I want a list of all the people who were taken."

"Yeah, I'll get that," Adam mumbled, and I turned to him.

"You *want* to stop breathing," I commanded him. His body immediately stiffened, and his eyes enlarged. A hand slapped against his chest, and he looked around the room as he realized what I had done. I approached him, glaring at him. "You will never keep something like this from me again. Do you understand me?"

Adam only stared at me, his face turning pale as his lips began to move up and down like a fish out of water.

"You are not the Master; you do not keep anything from me.

Do you understand me, Adam? Do not think you are special; I can take you out in a second and replace you."

Adam nodded, his eyes almost bulging from their sockets. I snapped my fingers, "Breathe."

Adam sucked in a massive lungful of air, bending at his waist and coughing as he expelled what was in his lungs and sucked in more oxygen.

"Now, tell me what you know about the missing people."

He straightened. "We aren't the only ones missing people. I heard the mistress is missing them too."

"You have? Do you know how many?"

"I don't know, but probably about the same as us, maybe more. She does have more followers." The instant he said that, his eyes enlarged, and he stepped back as if he expected me to do something. It wasn't worth my effort.

"Do we know where they are or what they are doing?"

"No, we don't. There was talk that it was humans—"

I scoffed at him. "Humans? You must be joking? Why would they come after our people?"

Adam shrugged again. "Don't know, and I'm not saying it is humans. I'm just saying what I've heard. We have no idea who is taking people, or where they go."

"Do we have anyone working on this?"

"No, not really."

"Then I want people working on this, and a list of everyone who is missing. I want to know every detail that you have, and then some. You have until tomorrow to get it together."

"But, sir," Adam started to say, and I glared at him. "As you request, Master. We will have it for you tomorrow. Is there anything else you need?"

I sighed as I sank into a chair. "No buts. We need to get this figured out quickly. I can't have this messing up my plans. I've waited too damn long for this."

"Does he know yet?"

"Who, Zander? I believe he is figuring it out. Gabe told him about it the other night, and Laura said he has been unnaturally quiet and avoiding her. So he must be trying to protect himself. I think he figured out that she could remove his thoughts."

"Think he remembers me killing him?"

I grinned at him. "I don't know; would you like me to ask him? Maybe he'd like to return the favor."

Adam shifted back. "No, sir. You don't have to ask him."

"Good idea. We will learn what Zander remembers and what he doesn't soon. In the meantime, I am giving him space to figure it out. Once I know he is ready for more, I'll make my move."

"Yes, sir."

"I believe you have work to get done, Adam. Get me that information."

"Yes, sir. I will."

I watched Adam leave and then leaned back in my seat, filling my mouth with the whiskey and savoring it. Where were my people disappearing to? Was it possible they had fled to start a new rebellion? Had they possibly returned to the side of the mistress?

I was going to have to reach out to my sources, see who knew what. I had two sets of eyes at the mistress' headquarters; which one should I reach out to? Probably not Hugh, he was too young and just becoming acclimated to our world. I'm sure he probably didn't know much. I guess I was going to have to reach out to the other one.

I did wonder how the mistress' son was doing these days.

CHAPTER TWENTY-THREE

ANGELINA

*A*fter the guys left to speak with Hugh's boss, I went back upstairs. Kristin was in her office, and I went to her corner bar, opened the small fridge, and removed a blood bag, pouring it into a crystal glass as she stared at a computer screen.

I didn't think she was really looking at it; her eyes weren't moving, and the screen wasn't changing.

"Earth to Kristin," I said as I took a seat across from her.

She blinked slowly and shifted her eyes to mine. Her irises were gray today, but of course, she wasn't happy.

"What did you say?"

"I said, where is your mind?"

"I was trying to feel Joshua."

"No luck?"

"No. You know what it feels like when a life force snaps that you are bound to?"

I snorted, remembering Leo from way back when. "Yeah."

"I can still feel that, so I know he's not dead. He's just someplace that he is totally blocked off."

"So, are you thinking jail cell with metal walls?"

"Yeah, that is exactly what I'm thinking." She tapped her nails on the desktop. "It reminds me of when Alex was kidnapped by Burke."

I shifted in my seat; I'd been involved in that one. "Sorry."

She shrugged. "Maybe we should start looking into what the humans are building recently."

I laughed. "Yeah, what state do you want to start in, Kris? We are in Philly; they could have a warehouse in Northern New York, or out west."

"I don't think they are that far. The people that are missing are from Virginia up through New York and as far west as Ohio, but that's it."

"I didn't realize it was localized. How did you figure that out?"

"Mick and I went through the files again."

"Ah." I grinned at her over my glass. "You put your detective hat back on, huh?"

She chuckled. "Yes, I did, and to be honest, it felt good. Been a while since I was involved in an investigation and not dealing with the administrative side of things."

"You should try to do more of it then."

She rolled her eyes. "The only reason I'm doing it now is because of Josh."

"You do know that you control what you do and don't do, right? I mean, it's not like you have to ask the boss or anything."

"Funny, Lena."

"Have you heard from Hugh?"

"I heard from Cameron. He said Hugh did really good, even compelled his boss."

"He what?"

"Yep, Cameron explained what to do, and Hugh did it. His eyes even shifted color."

"Holy shit! Maybe that is a reborn thing."

"I don't know. My eyes used to shift colors back when I was

Calista, although not as drastically."

"True, but my eyes shift when I am breaking compulsion or helping you."

"Then maybe it does have something to do with it. Since we don't know any other reborns, we can't test that yet."

"What do you mean, yet?"

She sighed and studied me carefully. "It means, I am actively searching now."

"Is that why I had to give Emily my blood?"

"Yes."

"But we already know that I'm a reborn."

"Yes, and I am too, and so is Hugh. I am having our blood tested to see what is different about it from the rest of our breed. It's about time we study this and figure it out. Maybe it can tell us why our blood is caustic to others, or when it turned that way. Maybe we'll know with Hugh and be able to track it."

"And maybe if we test humans, we might find some other reborns that aren't aware."

"Yes, but I have to figure out how to test humans. It's not like I can go around asking for their blood."

"No, that wouldn't be good." I stared at my almost empty glass, and then my eyes jumped to hers. "I think I have an idea."

"What's that?"

"The other day I was thinking about how it would be great to have a dance club in the hotel. We have the room here. That back ballroom is barely ever used. We could convert it to a club; it even has a separate entrance around the back of the building that we could dress up to make it look fancy."

"Why would we want a club here?"

"Because we saw how awesome it was when you left the building. People got killed. If we had a club here, we could work off some steam, and we could check the humans that came in. Maybe we require them to give us a fingerprint when they enter, and we prick their finger and take a blood sample."

I could see Kristin chewing on that, but before she could answer, the door burst open and in walked Hugh, Cameron, Ryker, and Conner—all of which were grinning like fools.

"I gotta tell you, Mistress, this guy is gonna be something," Ryker said as he plopped down into a chair.

"Why, because he could compel someone?" I asked.

Cameron shrugged. "Yeah, but because he did it so well, we already have some information."

"What?" Kristin demanded as Hugh paused by her desk and stared down at her. She nodded to him, and he bent forward and kissed her.

Aww, so sweet—blech.

"We don't know the exact location, but Steve called me as we were getting back to the hotel and told me that there is a holding facility somewhere in eastern Ohio," Hugh told her as he stood upright.

My sister turned to me. "And now we have a place to search." She stood. "Can you all excuse Hugh and me for a few minutes?"

Everyone started heading back to the door, and I sighed. Kristin looked at me. "I'll meet you down in that ballroom in about fifteen minutes. Let's talk it over. Get anyone you think would be good to work on it with you, and have them there. Hugh can help you with that too."

"Help with what?" Hugh asked.

I ignored him as I asked my sister, "You're serious?"

"Absolutely. I think it's a fantastic idea." She stated the next part into my mind. *"But do not tell anyone about the blood yet."*

"Awesome!" I said as I turned and followed Ryker and Conner out.

"What are you working on?" Cam asked as we headed down the hall.

"I'm trying to talk my sister into opening a club here in the hotel."

"A club?"

"Yes, a nightclub." I stopped beside the elevator. "You didn't see her the night we went out, Cam. She was so much like her old self. She was having fun. When is the last time she was able to really have fun? Forty, twenty-five, eighteen years ago? She needs this."

He chuckled. "I think you might need this too."

"I do. I'm not going to lie about that. I could totally do with some fun around here. I'm tired of wandering around here and not having anything to do while we wait for the other shoe to drop."

"Speaking of shoes." The elevator opened, and we stepped in after Lainey exited. Rex stood in the corner and nodded. "Did Kristin come up with anything here?"

"No, not really. She wanted to start looking around, but we didn't have an area. Now we have an area where we can start. Ohio is a little smaller than the entire U.S."

Rex jumped in. "We know where he is?"

"No, we have a possible location, Rex, but it's a really big area."

"Can she feel Josh?"

"No, she can't. She knows he's not dead, but she can't tell more than that. He's probably in a cell of some kind."

"Those fucking humans, man, wait till we locate them. I will be first in line to wipe them all out."

Cameron studied Rex. "You know, you sound a lot like Portage right now."

"I'm nothing like Portage, Cameron. Don't insult me like that. I know that not all humans are trash, but these guys are, and they need to be put back in their place."

"Put back in their place?" I echoed back. "Rex, you do know that there are more of them around than there are of us, and that they have been here longer."

"Do we really know that? What if we were the first to exist?"

"Jesus, Rex, why are we even talking about this. Look, your

mother is trying to locate Joshua and the rest of the missing breed members. Once she does, I'll make sure you get to go rescue your bestie." I smiled wickedly at him, and he grumbled under his breath as the door opened, and he slipped out.

I sighed as I exited, Cameron's hand on my lower back. "He's worse than his father. At least Trent was nice most of the time and could have fun. Rex is just irritable all the time."

"Give the kid a break; he just found out that he is not in line to take over after his mother, and I heard Novah dumped him."

I glanced at him. "What do you know about that?"

"I know that Novah is hooking up with someone else now." Cameron kept his eyes facing forward.

"You see that in someone's mind?" I asked.

He laughed. "I see everything in people's minds. I honestly wish that I didn't. It's getting old."

"Yeah, well, Novah is old; she should know better than to hook up with men half her age."

Cameron's face snapped my way. "You knew?"

"Yes, I went to see Garrett, and she was there."

"What do you think of that?" he asked as we headed down the hallway toward the ballroom.

I glanced around. "I think she's trying to get her hooks into any man that can help her achieve something. I'm not sure what that something is, but I don't trust her."

"She won't even stay in the same room as me." He laughed. "When I show up someplace, she hightails it out. Makes her look even more guilty."

"Yes, it does." We stepped into the ballroom, and the two of us looked around.

"If we insulated the walls better, we could soundproof this area so it wouldn't bother the rest of the hotel," Cam said.

"Yes, that's true. Do you think we could put a second level in here?"

"You mean a second floor?"

"Yeah, a balcony of types, where Kristin could come in and see what is going on without having to meander among the other people."

Cameron laughed. "I think the ceiling is high enough that you might be able to put a second-floor VIP section."

"Perfect!" I clapped my hands together and did a double take at Cam when I saw him staring at me. "What?"

He gave me a small smile. "Nothing, I forgot how pretty you are sometimes."

I snorted a laugh and stepped away from him. "Yeah, okay, Cam. No reason to butter me up; you've already gotten me into bed."

He grabbed my arm and pulled me back around so quickly that I lost my footing and fell against him. "You know, I see what's going on inside your mind, too, Lena. I know how much you want Hugh, and how you are fighting the jealousy of your sister."

"I am not jealous of my sister."

He shrugged. "Maybe not her job, but you are of her mating."

I could choose to ignore his comment, but he would only look at that as a sign of guilt. "Okay, so I'm jealous of what she has found. That doesn't mean I want him for myself."

"Oh, yeah?" Cameron said as his ran his fingers up my arm. "You sure about that? I saw that scene on the roof where you were watching, and you definitely wanted to take part."

I shoved Cameron back. "Stay the fuck out of my head, Cameron. You do not have the right to be in there."

"I can't help it that your thoughts are loud, and the bond that we shared is still there—however slight it is—Lena."

"Yeah, well, we need to find a way to break that bond. I'm tired of you digging around in my skull." I walked away from him.

"Angelina, I didn't mean to upset you. I was mostly joking about Hugh."

I twisted around, hiking a brow. "Mostly?"

"Yeah, well, I can't help feeling a little jealous myself when I see you wanting another man."

I was back in his face before he could blink. "That is your own fault, Cameron. You are the one that left me! You walked away from me to play house with Rosa! I didn't do anything to chase you off. I thought what we had was good, but I must have been delusional."

This was the first time in a long time that Cameron and I had spoken about this. While I tried to hide it, I still held anger at him for leaving me all those years ago.

"It was good, Angelina. I was the problem, not you. I'm sorry for what I did."

I laughed. "Oh, it's the it's not you, it's me speech. How quaint."

Cameron grabbed my face, pulling me closer so that our noses almost touched. "Angelina, I loved you then, and I still love you now. I broke our bond because I was scared. I saw what happened to Trent and how Kristin's blood changed him, and I could feel things happening inside of me, and I didn't like them. I knew it was your blood, and I didn't want to do what Trent did, because I knew what it would do to you! I left to protect us both. I didn't do it because I didn't love you, but because I did love you."

My jaw dropped. "You could feel my blood changing?"

"Yes."

"And it was affecting you?"

"Yes."

"You left because you didn't want to hurt me by killing yourself?"

He nodded, and I shoved him away. "You son of a bitch! You should have told me that thirty years ago! All these years, you made me think that I wasn't desirable enough for you, but it was my blood that wasn't desirable! Damn you, Cameron Fields!"

CHAPTER TWENTY-FOUR

ZANDER

I hadn't slept well in a few days because my mind was too active. It was constantly switching back and forth between past and present, and I was trying to make sense of it all. How was it possible to have all these memories of a man named Julian when I had never met the man?

Was I somehow cosmically connected to him in some odd way? As the days had passed, more memories filled my mind, but not just memories—feelings too. It was like I could feel every single thing that this man had felt. I could not only hear the voices and see the faces but the emotions that went with them.

Laura's friend Gabe was a considerable part of those memories. He was almost everywhere, along with Alexander Armstrong. Julian and Gabe had worked together, but they were also friends. The friendship that this Julian shared with Alex was most likely why I had wanted to get involved when my father was torturing him. I had always wondered if it was to assist or stop it. Now, I believed it was to stop it.

During many of the memories, the mistress would appear, but she wasn't a mistress then. She was merely Kristin, and I learned a lot about the younger woman from those thoughts that appeared in my mind.

Kristin Greene or I guess I should say, Officer Kristin Greene was a small-town cop. My thoughts on her changed almost daily. At times I would feel so much passion for her that it was daunting. Another time, I would be angry. So angry that it was hard to do anything else, and then there were times where grief overwhelmed me.

The snippets of memories that I had recalled earlier made more sense now. Much more of those short scenes had come forward and filled in the blanks, but I still had significant vacant areas and a whole lot of questions. The problem was, I didn't know who to ask.

It was obvious that my father had been trying to keep whatever the hell this was quiet—or from me. In fact, he was the one that found Laura and set up the introduction. It was him that urged me to get to know her better, to invite her to move in with me, to bond with her. All so that she could oversee my thoughts, report back to him, and for what reason? What was his objective?

Was it possible that he knew who this Julian was? I had to think that he did since Alexander, his brother, had worked so closely with Julian. But how would he know that I would have some connection to Julian? Had he manufactured it somehow? Was this some weird vampire power?

My mind came back to Gabe. He was the one that told me about Julian. The one that had said the names that had started the ball rolling. Did he know why I had memories of his friend and him, and so many other people?

He had to. The intense way he had watched me as if waiting to see what would happen. The way he had brought up the conversation that to anyone else, would have meant nothing, but to me—to us—was crucial to whatever was going on with me.

I had to find Gabe. He was the only one that I could think to talk to, except maybe Kristin—Kristin. The mere thought of her brought a longing so deep to my soul that I had trouble breathing for a moment. I didn't understand it, didn't know if I even wanted to understand it. She was the enemy.

Or was she?

Could I just pick up the phone and call her? Ask her about this? Maybe show up on her doorstep? No, that wasn't an option, not with who my father was.

I stood staring out at the water; the ebb and flow of the waves did nothing for me tonight as I thought of the man that raised me. Was it my father that was the enemy? Was he even my father? Everything I knew in my life right now I was questioning.

I growled to the night air in frustration right before I heard a transport coming down my drive toward my house. Was Laura finally coming back? Would she somehow manage to wipe my mind clear, make me forget everything? This time I was ready for her. For the last few days, I've been writing things down, like a lot of things that I have seen in my mind. If she took them away, this time, I would be able to remember them.

I heard the door to the transport open and close, but I didn't feel Laura. I felt someone else, and for the first time in a few days, I was looking forward to something. I moved back into my house and toward the door, yanking it open as a man paused on the other side.

I stared at him for a long time, and then he finally spoke. "I bet you have a lot of questions."

"I do." I stepped back and let Gabe cross the threshold and then closed the door. "Can I get you a drink?"

"Yeah, I could use one."

I went to my bar and poured us each a drink. After handing his off to him, I took a seat on the white leather couch. "Have a seat."

He sipped from his glass and smiled reminiscently as he looked at it, then he sank to the chair behind him. "The real stuff."

"Yeah, no fake shit for me."

"I used to drink this all the time with Julian."

"I think I knew that." We stared at one another. "Why do I know that?"

"Because you are Julian."

I frowned at him. "I can't be Julian. I'm Zander Portage. I remember my entire life, and until recently, I never even heard the name Julian before."

Gabe inhaled deeply. "You are what is called a reborn."

"A what?"

"A reborn. You know how we stake our dead?"

"Of course, to turn them to ash."

"Yeah, so they can't be reborn."

"What are you talking about?"

"Listen for a minute, Zander. I'll explain." He sipped from his glass again. "If you die and you are not staked at the time of your death, then your soul is reborn into another person created at that moment. You will carry their genes, their memories, sometimes even their looks and scents."

"That's not possible."

"It is! Look inside your memories at Kristin; she was Calista! She was a reborn. You were mated to Calista about eighty years ago, and she died a few years into your mating, along with your daughter, Anastasia. Calista came back as Kristin; Anastasia came back as her twin sister, Angelina. You were Julian; you died and came back as Zander."

"That's fucking impossible," I said, but deep inside, this was making some weird kind of sense. I do remember scenes with a woman named Calista, who was so very much like Kristin, yet oddly different, and there had been a child in a few odd memories.

A vicious scene exploded into my mind. The feelings of fear, anger, and failure as someone watched a child having their neck torn open, a woman screaming, a man with vicious blue eyes glaring at me—Damon. His name was Damon.

Suddenly, it shifted to another scene, and Kristin was dressed in her police uniform, rushing for the door, a sweet, creamy scent in the air as she fled the room. Julian was watching from the window, speaking to a woman behind her. Gabe was there too.

"It's her, isn't it, Gina Marie?" The words were soft, and Julian had closed his eyes, turning everything dark for a moment.

"I believe it is, Julian," the woman said.

"Who is she supposed to be?" Gabe asked.

Julian turned to face the woman—Gina Marie—her name came to me immediately. Her husband, Brendon, was watching Julian—me?

"How long have you known?" Julian asked.

"Ten years ago, I saw her. The moment I spoke with her, I thought it had to be her. It was only when I saw the two of you together that I was absolutely positive. I know you are wondering why I didn't find you and tell you, but she was young, so far from being ready for our culture, and she was involved with a human. I wasn't sure if it was too late, and I didn't want to hurt you if it was." Gina Marie smiled sadly. "How long did it take you to figure it out?" she asked Julian.

"Who is she supposed to be?" Gabe asked again, looking eager to be part of the conversation.

"Instantly...I knew it the moment her scent entered my nose. I knew it was Calista..."

I blinked back to the present. "Kristin was Calista?"

Gabe nodded. "Yes, and that second scene was the day that you found out she was back. I saw the scenes in your head just now. Until that day, it had been a rumor, and we'd never really known for sure that it could happen, but it did. Kristin was almost identical to Calista."

I stared at him, my mind trying to digest this new information. Was I a reincarnation of myself?

"You don't look the same, but your eyes are identical. That was the one feature that both Kristin and Calista adored about you—your eyes. You smell the same, too—cinnamon and leather. When you and Kristin were in the same room, people always got hungry for cinnamon buns."

"I've seen her say things about my eyes," I replied, and Gabe nodded.

"How is this possible?" I asked him.

Gabe shrugged. "I don't know. I don't know how it works."

"Do you know how Julian died, why he wasn't staked?"

Gabe frowned. "Yeah, a guy that worked with you—Julian, not Zander—killed you in the woods. Kristin was there, she saw it. He slit your throat and then pushed you backward over a cliff, and Kristin said she felt your lifeline snap as you fell."

"Did she kill the guy?"

He shook his head slowly. "No."

"Who was it?"

"I don't know. She never told me."

"Do you still talk to Kristin?"

His shoulders rose and fell with a heavy sigh. "No, we had a falling out a few years back."

I studied him carefully. "Enough of a falling out that you changed sides?"

"Let's just say that my mate got a wee bit out of control, and Kristin had to put her foot down. I don't agree with a lot of what your father stands for, but I don't think human-turned should be banished or put to death, and there are quite a few good human-turned out there."

"Does he know that you were close to Kristin?"

"Yes."

"Has he asked you to do anything against her?"

"Not yet, but I'm pretty sure he will."

"What are you going to say to him?"

Gabe stared at me hard. "That depends on how you feel about it."

"What are you talking about?"

"Are you prepared to learn who you really are, Zander?"

Was I? Would what I learn change my life? Of course, it would. Did I want that? Had I not been sitting around for thirty-five fucking years wondering what the hell my purpose was? Could this be it? I shifted to the edge of the couch.

"Yes, I'm ready to learn more about Julian and how we are connected."

Gabe seemed to relax slightly, and that was probably because he was worried that I would do something like strike him dead. Hardly an option when he appeared to be the only one on my side right now.

"Good."

"What do I do?"

Gabe stood, digging into his pocket and removing a piece of paper. "Saturday at five, get away from here. Pack only what you can carry in a small backpack. I will have a transport get you after you call the number on that. After you call it, destroy that piece of paper."

"Where is it going to take me?"

Gabe smiled. "It's going to take you back to where it all started—Fawn Hollow, Pennsylvania."

"Why there? What am I going to find there?"

"Hopefully, you will find your past and connect with your future."

"My future? How do you know my future?"

Gabe shook his head. "I don't. All I can do is hope that you connect with it, and connect quickly."

He set his drink down, handed me the paper, and stared at me really hard as if he were trying to tell me something. I let down my mental wall for a moment. *"Bond immediately—*

trust me!" he whispered, and then he rushed out of the house.

I stared at the open door and then at the paper in my hand. I unfolded it and read the number and the words underneath. "Bond immediately!"

I frowned and went to shut the door. Bond with what?

CHAPTER TWENTY-FIVE

HUGH

*W*e were almost back to the hotel when my cellphone rang, and I saw Steve's number on it. Instead of putting it on virtual, I put the phone to my ear. "I didn't expect you to call so quickly, Steve."

"Yeah, well, neither did I. I think you were right, Hugh. I think they are collecting some of the more special vampires and locking them up."

"Do you know where?"

"All I could find out was it was in Ohio."

"Why are they doing it?"

Steve sighed. "Are you really one of them?"

"Yes, I am. Now tell me why they are kidnapping the vampires."

"Because they want to use the special ones to control the rest of you."

"Control the rest of us? How?"

"I don't know, but they want to keep you in line. They think that if they have the most powerful ones under their control, they can control the rest of you."

"There is no way they can control them—us," I stated. "Did you learn anything else?"

"Hugh," his voice sounded strained, "if I tell you anything else, my family is going to be in jeopardy. I know you can do some mind control thing, and I have to do what you say because I want to spill my guts right now, but I have to protect my family."

Cameron put his hand out as if he were asking for the phone, and I passed it over to him.

"Steve, this is Cameron. We appreciate your fast work, so much so that we are going to protect your family. Have them pack a bag for a few days, and we will have someone pick you up and take you someplace safe."

I could hear Steve's voice easily from where Cameron held the phone. "What? You're going to kidnap us?"

"No, not at all. We are going to keep you and your family safe. Despite some of the rumors that you might have heard, we do not want to hurt you, your family, or other humans."

"How do I know you can do that?" He paused. "Wait, why do I need you all to protect me?"

Cameron chuckled. "Steve, you just started asking questions, and as soon as they find out that Hugh is one of ours—not yours—they are going to know something is up. Besides, you just told Hugh that if you say anything more, your family is going to be in harm's way. Consider us your personal security team."

"Give me the phone back," I said to Cam. He handed it back to me, and I put it to my ear. "Steve, you know me. I am not going to let anything happen to you, Valerie, or the kids."

"Hugh, you have more integrity than any man I know, so I'm going to trust you on this, but I'm also going to tell you that I don't like it."

"Copy that, sir. Get yourself packed; we'll have someone pick you up soon."

I hung up the phone and studied the back of Cameron's head. "And why did we just offer him protection?"

"Because he's afraid of something—which means he knows something. Either he knows details, or he knows people. Both of those we can use to our advantage."

"I guess that is very true," I replied, and Conner and Ryker filled the silence with talk of a football game they had seen. We all went straight up to Kristin's office and inside. Her sister didn't look all that happy to see us, but I was kind of flying high as Ryker spoke to Kristin.

"I gotta tell you, Mistress; this guy is gonna be something."

"Why, because he could compel someone?" Angelina asked like it was no big deal. Maybe to her it wasn't a big deal, but a week ago, I sure as hell couldn't imagine being able to do that.

"Yeah, but because he did it so well, we already have some information."

"What?" Kristin asked as I stopped beside her desk.

"Am I allowed to kiss you hello? Or is that not appropriate?"

She snickered into my head. *"Kissing is almost always appropriate."*

I winked at her as I leaned forward and gave her just a single tender kiss. *"I'm ready to have you alone again."*

"Insatiable—I love it." She laughed briefly.

"For you, oh, hell yeah!" I forced myself to return to business. "We don't know the exact location, but Steve called me as we were getting back to the hotel and told me that there is a holding facility somewhere in eastern Ohio."

Kristin looked at her sister. "And now we have a place to search." She stood. "Can you all excuse Hugh and me for a few minutes?"

Everyone was making their way to the door when she told her sister that she'd meet her downstairs soon. Guess I wasn't going to get a quickie like I thought—damn.

The minute the door closed, Kristin spun on me. The heated

look in her eye told me that I had been wrong. I was totally going to get my quickie. I speared my hand into her hair and yanked her head back, putting my mouth to her neck where my fangs had already lowered. Her body quivered against mine, and I scooped her up, set her on the desk, and broke the skin in one fluid movement. She worked at my zipper, whimpering as I sucked deeply from her neck, and freed me in record time as I pushed her skirt up to her hips. One quick thrust and I was sheathed deeply in her, and she turned her face to my wrist and latched on.

The sex was hard, quick, and deliciously satisfying. Kristin removed her fangs from my wrist and then slowly kissed my neck as I released her vein. "Why is it always so awesome?"

She chuckled. "Actually, I think it's better for me."

"Not possible," I said as I took her face and kissed her slowly.

"Imagine not having someone drinking from your vein," she said, and I frowned.

"How long has it been?"

"Since anyone had more than a sip? Ten years I think."

I stared at her. I could not imagine having sex with her and not taking her vein. "That's because your blood is different."

"Yes, as is yours."

"True, but mine isn't dangerous right now. So if I wanted to share it with someone else, I could. Not that I want to, but I'm just asking."

"Yes, yours should be safe." She paused and chewed on her lip. "Although I'm not sure after you've had mine. I don't know if that will speed up the process of yours."

"Speed up the process?"

She stared at me as if she were trying to decide something, then smiled. "Yeah, who knows." Somehow I got the feeling that she had wanted to say something else but was holding back. Did she not trust me?

"Hey." I stared deep into her eyes, trying to get into her closed mind, but it was like Fort Knox. "Do you trust me, Kris?"

"Do I have a reason not to trust you, Hugh?"

I shook my head. "Absolutely not. I have been nothing but honest and trusting with you."

"I'm glad to hear that." She shifted on the desk, pushing me back. "And as awesome as that little snack was, I need to get back to work."

"Yeah, you said you needed to go meet your sister downstairs, and I could help her with something? What do you have in mind?"

We straightened our clothing, and I waited as Kristin stepped into her bathroom for a moment and then returned. "Angelina wants to put a dance club into the hotel. I think it's a good idea. We need some fun around here, and I can't be running out every couple of days to make sure everyone is entertained."

"Really?" I said excitedly. "I think that would be great!" Kristin started to pass me, and I grabbed her arm and spun her toward me. "Does this mean I'll finally get to dance with the Mistress?"

Her head rolled back on her shoulders as she laughed, and I found myself grinning at her. I liked the carefree Kristin. "I think we can arrange that."

"Sounds like a deal," I said as I stared down at her.

"How did it feel to compel someone?" she asked.

"Pretty awesome. Could I compel you?"

"Um, not sure, we can try it sometime, but not today." She pulled out of my arms. "Right now, I need to get downstairs and listen to Angelina's ideas."

"Wait, I forgot to tell you something."

"What's that? Can we talk on the way?"

"Yeah." We started toward the elevator. "My boss and his family are going to be here at the hotel."

"Why?"

"Well, because I compelled him to ask questions, and now that he has, when word gets out that I'm playing for the other team, he could be in danger."

"Possibly" she said as she hit the button. I glanced back and found Jett and Paxton standing behind us. I nodded at them. The elevator opened, and we all stepped in.

"Can I keep talking?" I asked her, and she glanced at Jett and Paxton.

"Yep, they are glued to my hip right now, so talk away." I chuckled, and Jett and Paxton both grinned back at me.

"Cam seems to think that my boss might know more than he is saying."

"I'm sure he does, and if he is feeling safe and feels like we can protect him, he might tell us."

"Yeah, that's what Cam was thinking."

"Makes sense. Do we have people picking them up?"

"Yeah, Cameron set it up as soon as we got back."

"Good." The elevator opened again, and we all headed out. The lobby of the hotel was packed, and I paused and looked around in surprise. Everyone turned to gape at us, and Kristin laced her hand with mine, smiled at everyone, and then led me around the corner—Paxton and Jett close on our heels.

"What was that all about?"

"Curiosity," she said. "I told you before; you are big news. Everyone wants to see the newest reborn, and my mate."

I laughed. "Never saw myself as a celebrity."

Kristin snorted roughly. "Yeah, well, neither did I."

"Were they all vampires?"

"You should figure that out on your own," she replied.

"How do you do that?"

"Humans feel different. Their hearts beat differently, faster, and they smell different."

"You know, I noticed at my boss' house when my fangs came

out that I could almost taste his blood in the air, like the scent was stronger suddenly."

"Exactly."

Jett stepped around us and pulled open the door, and we stepped in to find Angelina screaming at Cameron.

"You son of a bitch! You should have told me that thirty years ago! All these years, you made me think that I wasn't desirable enough for you, but it was my blood that wasn't desirable! Damn you, Cameron Fields!"

Both of them looked flustered that we had walked in on that, but Kristin didn't seem fazed. She walked right past them and glanced around. "Do you think it's big enough?"

Cameron had taken a deep breath, glanced my way, and then replied to Kristin. "Lena and I were discussing the possibility of adding a second floor in here, like a VIP lounge. That way you, or others, could watch from above."

Kristin grinned at her sister a little wickedly. "You planning on having a glass stage too?"

Angelina laughed as if we hadn't just walked in on a very personal argument. "Nice idea, but we need something else to gather attention. We don't want to duplicate Dangers."

"True, but I do like that stage."

They grinned at each other as if sharing a secret. Then Angelina and Kristin started talking details like where the DJ would be. What about a stage? How many bars would they need? How much seating and so on. Cameron and I listened and gave input as requested, but for the most part, we remained quiet.

Rex stepped into the ballroom as they were about to finish up. "What are you doing down here?" he asked his mother, totally ignoring me.

"Working, did you need something, Rex?"

"Yeah, I need to know when we are going to get Joshua back."

"When we locate him, we will."

"I thought you knew where he was."

"We only know that he is in Ohio. We don't know where or what kind of a facility he is in."

"Shouldn't we have people preparing to go?"

Kristin turned to face him fully, stepping closer to him. "And do what, Rex? Get close enough to get caught so that we have to find a way to get more people out?"

"We should be getting ready, not talking about redecorating," he growled.

The door opened off to the side, and Ryker stuck his head in. "Hugh, your boss is here."

I faced Kristin as she said, "You get them comfortable, put them on the sixth floor, tell Trena at the front desk that I said the VIP apartment."

"Okay, I'll catch up with you later." I was heading out when I heard Rex question her.

"Isn't his boss a human? Why are we putting a human in one of our VIP apartments?"

I pursed my lips. Rex was a pain in the ass, but luckily, not my problem. He had been like a spoiled teenager ever since I had first seen him in the lounge the first night I came here. I knew I was nothing to him, but I wondered if I could get away with putting him over my knee and spanking him. I was pretty sure that the guy hadn't ever had that happen to him.

CHAPTER TWENTY-SIX

KRISTIN

"*I*sn't his boss a human? Why are we putting a human in one of our VIP apartments?" Rex snapped at me like he was entitled to an answer.

"This attitude right here, buster, is why you will never be the master, Rex. You do not demand answers; you help find solutions. You don't throw your weight around; you weigh the choices and see which one will better fit a situation. Get the stick out of your ass and stop acting like a spoiled teenager."

"I am trying to find solutions! I'm trying to figure out how we are going to get Joshua back."

"Is it just Joshua that you want back, Rex? You do know that there are a lot more people missing besides Josh," Angelina commented. "Something going on between you two that we don't know about?"

"No!" he hissed. "He's important to us, to her!" He pointed a finger at me as if saying my name was not possible. I rolled my eyes.

"I'm going to answer your earlier question because it has to do with what I'm doing, but Hugh's boss is the one that found out the general location of the facility. We believe he knows more, but he's afraid to talk because they might come after him. We have offered our protection in hopes that he will share what he knows."

"Then let's go find out!" he spouted. "Let me talk to him; I'll get him to answer me."

I was in his face a second later, lifting him by the throat. "You will do no such thing, Rex. You will back the fuck off and calm down. You will find something to keep yourself busy, and then when the time is right, I will allow you to assist with freeing Joshua and the other breed members who have been taken."

His face was turning red, but he didn't struggle. He knew better. I set him down. "Now go find something to do. In fact, find Lainey and start working with her. I want to know anything special that our agents have dealt with in Ohio in the last two years. Gather it, go through it, and see me in my office at four."

He nodded but didn't speak before he turned and fled the room, steam practically billowing out of his ears.

"That boy," Angelina commented.

"Is as hardheaded as his father," I finished tartly.

Cameron laughed and added, "Or his mother."

"Hey." I laughed at Cam. "I resemble that." I scanned the ball-room again. "I think you have plenty to work with, Angelina. Run with it."

"Sounds good. What are you going to do now?"

"I'm going to go to meet Hugh's boss and say hello." I glanced at Cam. "And thanks for helping Hugh out."

Cam chuckled. "Yeah, no problem. Have fun with that," he said as I started to step away, and then I turned back and looked between my sister and her former mate.

"Cam, could you really feel a difference in her blood?"

His gaze shot to Angelina and then back to mine where he lifted his shoulders a little higher. "Yeah, I did."

"Cameron, would you be willing to test something for me?"

"Sure, what?"

"Drink Angelina's blood."

"No!" my sister shouted.

"What?" he barked at the same time.

"I want you to drink her blood and see what you taste. See how it reacts to you."

"Kris! That could kill him."

"No, he'll be okay. If your blood hurts him, I can fix him."

"How the hell can you do that?" my sister asked with her hands on her hips and her eyes narrowed suspiciously.

"Trust me, okay? I can fix Cam." I turned back to Cameron. "Will you trust me?"

"Kris, if you want me to do that, I will." He didn't look all that excited, but he nodded. "How much do you want me to take?"

"Three mouthfuls," I stated.

"Have you lost your fucking mind?" Angelina erupted. "Joshua didn't take nearly that much from you, and it almost killed him."

"Trust me, Angelina. Cam will be fine."

"I'll do it."

"No, I won't let you," she growled at Cameron, but before she could say another word, Cameron was at her neck and biting down. My sister's head fell back, and she whimpered at the ecstasy.

I felt Cameron fighting the blood. Heard him take the final swallow and all but shove her away as he began to gag and dropped to his knees, his face turning fire engine red.

"Kristin!" Angelina screamed in panic.

"Relax, Angelina," I told her and went to my knees beside him, taking his wrist and putting it to my mouth.

Cameron looked up at me as he winced, his eyes tearing, and as I bit into his wrist, I felt his pain. Felt the burn of the blood deep in his gut. *Blood of mine, return to me.* As I sucked, I felt the blood responding, and Cameron stared at me in awe as I pulled a second time, calling to my blood one more time. As I did with Joshua, I left just a little bit of her blood still in him.

I released him, smiled at the amazed look on his face, and got to my feet.

"How did you do that?" he asked as he stared up at me. I glanced at my sister; she was as white as a sheet.

"I compelled my blood to return to me."

"What?" Angelina squeaked. "You can do that?"

Cameron struggled to get to his feet, but I helped him sit up, and then my sister came to his side to help him stand. "I learned that I could do that after Josh fed on me the last time. I had no idea that I could, but that wasn't the point. What did her blood taste like, Cam?"

"It tasted the same, incredible at first—but then it became a bit acidic once I swallowed. Then it was like battery acid, and it burned going down, but at the same time, the original flavor was still there, urging me to continue drinking."

"Okay, that's good to know."

He was still staring at me, and I began to step away, but he grabbed my arm. "Who knows that you can do that?"

"Only you two and Josh. You are only the second person I have tried it on."

Cam glanced over my shoulder, and I looked back to see Paxton and Jett there. "And them too now."

My sister snapped. "You are lucky it worked. I can't believe that you did that."

I eyed her carefully. "I did that for you. Next time, you can try it yourself. See if you can get it to return."

"Uh, no way!" she said as she stepped back and pulled Cameron with her, looking freaked out that I would even suggest that.

I chuckled and shrugged. "Your loss."

"My loss! What the hell does that mean?"

I shook my head and started to walk away. "I don't have time for this right now, Angelina. Figure out your own love life."

I blocked her out as I felt her preparing to blast me mentally. Jett and Paxton were waiting for me at the door. "Neither of you better say a word about what you saw."

"I saw nothing," Jett replied immediately with a slight smirk.

"Yeah, me either, except that was a pretty awesome nothing." She laughed softly.

I didn't respond to either of them, but I thought it was pretty awesome too.

We took the elevator up to the sixth floor and down to the suite that I had suggested Hugh take his boss to. It was more than just a hotel suite; it was a two-bedroom apartment. Ryker and Conner stood at the door, waiting for Hugh as it pulled open.

"I thought I felt you." Hugh winked and held the door open further.

I stepped in, leaving Paxton in the hall to wait, and nodded at Jett to accompany me inside. Hugh might trust these people, but I did not.

"I thought I would pop in and introduce myself to your boss and his family. Make sure that their accommodations were alright."

I stepped around him to find a man a few years older than him, attractive in a hard way, staring at me. Beside him was a woman, also attractive, but frightened and tired-looking, and on the couch were two children around the age of ten.

"You must be Steve Winwood." I held my hand out to him. I knew the human custom would put them at ease, and he readily took my hand and shook it. "My name is Kristin Armstrong."

"You're the mistress," his wife said quickly and then slapped a hand over her mouth.

I smiled at her and held my hand out to her. "Yes, I am, and I assume you are Steve's wife?"

"Yes." She took my hand cautiously. "Valerie and our sons, Duane and Donald."

I smiled at the kids, released her hand, and stepped back to give them space. "Well, I'm sorry for all the hustle and bustle tonight, but I believe you all will be comfortable here."

I glanced around and then back to Valerie as my eyes shifted color. "Might I suggest that you get the boys to bed?"

"Oh, yes, let me get the boys to bed. Come Duane, Donald, let's go check out your room." She hustled them from the room, and Steve studied me carefully.

"Did you do something to her?"

I gave him a kind smile. "I merely suggested something so that we could talk."

He turned to Hugh. "Did you do that to me earlier? When you—" He touched the side of his neck.

"When Hugh fed on you, yes, he did compel you. Your wife is tired and scared; she didn't need to be compelled. She just needed a suggestion. There is a difference."

"You didn't bite her though."

"I do not need to bite anyone to get them to do what I want, Steve."

He shifted back slightly. "How do I know that you will not hurt my family?"

"That is a fair enough question, and you have my word. Currently, I am one of the most powerful masters on the earth —if not the most powerful. People do not cross me without repercussion, and I do not harm people who do not deserve my wrath. Your family has not wronged me. As far as I know, you have not wronged me. I want your assistance and your word that you will be honest and helpful, and in return, your family will remain safe and sheltered."

"And if I don't?"

I smiled at him, the tips of my fangs peeking out from under my lips. "Then I won't be so nice—to you—I still won't harm your family. You might not know this about me, but once upon a time, I was a police officer, and I held life in the highest of regard. I still do, Steve, and I believe that your race and mine can live in harmony together without violence."

He looked at Hugh. "Can I trust her?"

Hugh stepped beside me and put his arm around my back. "Yes, Steve, you can. I trusted her with my life, and now, well, I'm a new person and her mate."

"Mate?"

"Like her husband." He shrugged.

"You're married to the mistress?" His gaze jumped to mine. "No offense."

"None taken. Get some rest, and we will talk later. I have some other business to attend to, but I hope that you continue to be honest and work with Hugh and Cameron."

I put my face up toward Hugh and waited for him to lean down and kiss me. "I'll see you later," I told him and then nodded to Jett, who opened the door and held it for me.

"You're really married to her?" I heard Steve ask as we reached the hallway.

"Yeah, I really am," Hugh responded with a chuckle as the door closed.

* * *

IT HAD BEEN DAYS, and while we had some ideas as to what part of Ohio the facility was in, we hadn't narrowed it down. Angelina and Cameron were busy with the club, and Hugh helped them when he wasn't helping me. Rex was still a significant pain in my ass, and Garrett was scarce. My understanding was that he was using his abilities to work during the day to see

215

what he could find with his human contacts—which at this point wasn't much.

I was still at my desk, staring at the map of Ohio that I had on my far wall when my gaze slipped over to the picture beside it. The photograph that sometimes lifted my spirits and other times flushed it down the toilet.

My cellphone rang, something it rarely did these days, and I glanced at the number to see one that I hadn't expected ever to see again. I hit the answer button. "Hello?"

His voice was soft, raspy. "Hey, sweet potato, you alone?"

I smiled briefly at his nickname from so long ago. "I am. Are you alright?"

"Not really, but I needed to tell you something."

I felt his stress through the line. "What's wrong, Gabriel?"

"Listen, have you ever wondered what happened to Julian?"

My eyes slammed back to the picture. "Why are you asking me that?"

"Have you?"

"Of course, I have, but he's dead. You know that."

"He's not."

I swear my heart skidded to a stop for a moment. I had been waiting for this moment for thirty-five years. "What?"

"He's alive."

I sat up slowly, my hands starting to shake slightly. "How do you know this?"

"Because I spoke to him. In fact, I helped him remember. He wants to see you. He has a lot of questions, questions that you will be able to answer. He needs to see you."

"Tell him to come here."

"I can't. He can't come there, but I set it up that he will meet you someplace. Just you, no one else. It's too dangerous right now."

"I can protect him."

"Not from this," he all but muttered. "Please, Kris, just meet him."

"I can't do that right now."

"Kris, you need to meet with him. This is Julian we are talking about. Your ultimate soulmate, and he needs your help."

I wanted nothing more than to drop everything and run to him, but how could I? Could I figure something out? "Where does he want to meet?"

"Your old home?"

"In Fawn Hollow?"

"Yes."

"When?"

"Late Saturday night, around three."

"Three? I can't get back here before sunrise then."

"Stay the night there. It's not like it doesn't have bedrooms."

"Why are you calling me to tell me this?"

"Because he was my best friend. He needs help; you can help him. I can't. This is the best that I can do. Please, just go see him." He sounded as if he were pleading with me.

"I'll try, but I can't promise anything."

"Kris, you owe me this. I need your help. Please, go see Julian."

"I said I would try."

"Remember how you would do anything for the people that you loved?" he said softly.

"That was a long time ago," I said just as softly.

"It's been a long time for you because you haven't loved anyone like you did since Julian died. He's back. Can you imagine what you two could accomplish now?"

Hugh's face came to mind, but I quickly brushed it aside as I stared at the picture on the wall. "Things are different. We aren't the same people."

"You don't know that. You and Julian were always magical

when you were together. Go to him, find out for yourself, please. I have to go. Be there at three, please."

The phone clicked, and he was gone. I stared at my phone for a moment and then shifted to my call log and deleted the call. No one needed to know that I had spoken with Gabe.

I set my phone down and approached the picture, staring at Julian's face and feeling the tiniest seed of hope spring to life. Are you really alive, Julian?

If there was a chance that he was, how could I refuse to go? I couldn't. I shifted my gaze to the map. If Julian was a reborn now, with my sister and Hugh, that made four of us. The possibilities were endless.

Hugh—ugh! I clenched my eyes for a moment. I couldn't think about him right now. I needed to figure out a way to get out of here and to Fawn Hollow without anyone knowing.

CHAPTER TWENTY-SEVEN

JOSHUA

his place was wicked, and I was so fucking over it. I had been here for several days—I think days, might have been hours or months—and spoken to no one. In fact, I hadn't even seen anyone outside the window except for the other people inside the cells across from me.

I wondered why I was never hungry. I hadn't eaten any food since I arrived, nor had I been given any blood. It was almost like my body was in some stasis mode and didn't need nourishment. Was I even awake? Was I in some warped sleep where my mind was making things up?

The walls were too thick to feel anything, and I could hear nothing but the sound of my own breathing and heartbeat. Every few hours, there were two short beeps and then a blast of electricity, or something similar, came out of the walls and knocked me on my ass.

The first couple of times that it had happened, I'd woken up on the floor of the cell, dazed and pissed off. Then I started to recognize the tones, and as soon as I heard them, if I were standing, I would lie down on my cot.

It would still nail me, but not as bad. It would also still knock me out, and I'd awaken pissed off all over again, but it didn't hurt as much. It was like when I was standing, I fought against it, and that made it hurt more.

It wasn't that I didn't want to fight, oh, hell, fucking yeah! I wanted to smash some skulls, drain a couple of dozen bodies, tear out every heart. These guys were going to pay, but I needed to bide my time and figure out who the hell these guys were first. So far the only thing I knew was they were sadistic bastards.

If there was anything that I had learned from Kristin, it was how to be patient. Forty years ago, she hadn't been all that patient, but after Alex had been killed, she had changed, as if overnight. Now she had more patience than any person I had ever known.

So I was trying to be like her. I was memorizing every sound, every vibration of this building. Sometimes the vibrations felt like large doors opening and closing—at least that is what I pictured in my mind. I wondered if they felt the same way for everyone.

If only there were a way to speak to the other people in here. I had tried everything from focusing on the person across from me to letting down every wall in my mind to see if someone else could reach me. Nothing—zip—zilch!

I had never felt so alone—so isolated—before, and it was driving me crazy. I think that was what they—whoever the fuck they were—were waiting for. They wanted us unbalanced, to break so that they could get intel out of us, or use us. Why else would they have brought us here? Were they planning on putting all of us into cells like this around the world, extinguishing our lives?

For a second, fear dripped into my veins. They could control us with that blast of electricity, so how easy would it be to turn it up and kill us with it? Wipe us all out in one fell swoop.

My heart thudded, and my palms grew damp. Was that what

they were trying to do? A vampire holocaust? The thought scared the crap out of me at the same time that adrenaline surged through my veins.

I had no doubt that Kristin and everyone else at the VMF were out searching for me. Kristin would never allow this to go, and when she found me, heads were going to roll. Now I was glad that she had Hugh at her side. With their combined strength, we might have a chance against this blast of whatever the hell it is!

A voice suddenly echoed through my chamber, and I rocketed into a sitting position, searching for the hidden speaker.

"I'd be interested in knowing what has made you so angry, Joshua Williams."

"You want to know? Why don't you come in here and we can have a little face-to-face chat? I'd be happy to tell you as I rip your heart from your chest."

He chuckled, the sound grating down my spine. "I don't think that is such a good idea, at least right now."

"Then fuck you!" I hissed at him.

"Such anger. I bet that helps you stay focused."

I lay down on my side, turning away from the speaker, assuming that there was also a camera watching me.

"Do you use that anger to protect your mistress?" My entire body tensed, but I didn't move otherwise. "No need to answer; I'm pretty sure I already know what it is. I've seen inside your head, Mr. Williams. I know how you feel about your mistress and her new mate. What if I told you I could help you?"

"Fuck off," I hissed and closed my eyes. I wasn't going to listen to a word he said. Whoever the fuck he was didn't deserve my attention.

"I can fix it so that her blood doesn't hurt you anymore. Wouldn't that be nice to finally have what you have desired for so long?"

He was lying. There was no way to fix that.

"I'm not lying," he stated, and my eyes popped open, wondering if he was still reading me. "I can fix you so that you can tolerate her reborn blood. That is what you call her, right? A reborn?"

My eyes closed again, and I crossed my arms over my chest tighter as I lay on my side, my back to the small window and open area of the cell.

"I'll let you think about that for a little while, Mr. Williams. Rest well now."

"Go to hell," I muttered, and then the two small beeps proceeded to echo through the room before my own blast of hell arrived and along with it the darkness.

CHAPTER TWENTY-EIGHT

ANGELINA

*M*y sister about gave me a heart attack, which wasn't possible for us, but still. She could have told us what she was going to do, but she didn't.

I watched her leave, and still agitated, I turned on Cameron and smacked him across the face.

"What the hell was that for?" he said as he put a hand to his cheek.

"For almost killing yourself! What if that hadn't worked, Cam? What a stupid thing to do!"

He took me by the shoulders, and I knew he could feel me still shaking. "It worked, Angelina, and if it had killed me, at least it would have been a good way to die."

I glared at him. "You're an idiot!"

"Who loves you."

Okay, so that deflated some of the anger, and I fell into his arms. "Cam, I thought you were going to die."

"I didn't, Lena, and that was pretty damn cool that she could call her blood back. I could literally feel it leaving my body."

I leaned back, studying him. "You could?"

"Yes, I could." He paused. "She left a little in me."

My eyes widened. "Why?"

"I think she wanted us to keep a bond. Which means you need to refresh your side of it."

I eyed him suspiciously. "Why?"

"I don't know, Lena, but Kris left just enough for us to lock on to one another. Maybe she did it for protection, I don't know, and I don't care. Refresh the bond, Lena." His words were husky as he finished, and he curled his hand around my neck and brought my mouth toward his neck. "Drink, Lena."

I wasn't one to look a gift horse in the mouth, and I latched on to his neck. I forced myself to control my urges, and after two swallows, I pulled back, feeling the connection between us.

"See, that wasn't so bad, was it?"

"Of course not," I muttered.

He inhaled and stepped away, and it was then that I realized he wasn't as calm and cool as he pretended. "That scared you, too, didn't it?"

"Yeah, a little bit."

I sighed, and he squeezed my arm. "I could wring her neck."

"You realize how cool of a weapon that can be, right, Angelina? We are going to need to figure out if you can do that too."

"I am not trying it on you!" I hissed.

"No, I wouldn't want you to. I'm still reeling from the pain of the last one. My insides are still knitting themselves together."

I frowned, and he chuckled. "I'm fine. I promise you. So what are your other thoughts about this club?"

I was appreciative of him changing the subject and trying to get my focus off of what had happened. Although in the back of my mind, I really wondered if I would be able to do that too.

I would have to speak to my sister, find someone to test it on. Make sure she was around so that in case it didn't work, she could fix it.

For the rest of the night, Cameron and several other people

worked with me to get the plans up and running on the club. With crews working twenty-four hours a day, we could get things done quickly. Of course, we'd need some assistance with permits and such, but with a little compelling here and there, we'd have it done in a couple of weeks.

* * *

CAMERON and I had fallen back into a pattern. We worked together during the day; we argued over little things, and then we fell together when our day was done. Our relationship had always been easy—until it wasn't.

"Any idea what is going on with your sister?" Cam asked as we lay in bed, sipping coffee that he'd just made.

I turned to him. "I didn't know something was going on."

"She's been locked down, like seriously locked down. I can't even see in her mind anymore, and I could always see. I'm not sure what she did, but she figured out how to block me, which makes me think she is up to something."

"Maybe that has to do with Hugh. Can you still read him?"

Cam laughed. "Oh, yeah. He might think he's blocking people, but his head is so all over the place. He's trying to put our affairs first, but there is a huge piece of him that still thinks like a human, worries about other people. He is worried about Kris too."

"Why is he worried about her?"

"She's been quiet with him for the last couple of days. She says nothing is wrong, but he can feel her turmoil. He thinks it has to do with Josh, but I don't think so. If it were Josh, she wouldn't hide it like she is. I think she knows something else."

"Huh." I gulped my coffee and then set my mug on the night-stand before I threw off the covers.

"Where are you going?"

"I'm going to talk with my sister."

He laughed. "I didn't mean to alarm you."

"You haven't alarmed me, but you're right. Kris has been distant, and I can't reach her. I know she's around, but I can't get into her head either."

"Okay, well, see if she will talk to you."

I leaned back over the bed, putting a kiss to his lips. "We'll see."

After getting dressed, I found Cameron gone, and I went straight to her apartment. I let myself in after saying hello to Jett and Paxton, who were waiting outside of her door, and paused.

Kristin was standing in the living room, staring at her shelf. I closed the door a little harder than usual, and she blinked and turned to me, sending me a smile that I knew was far from real.

"What are you doing?"

"Nothing." She walked away from the shelf and into her kitchen. I paused where she'd been standing and stared at the picture of her with Trent, Julian, and Alex. Which one was she missing?

"What have you been up to?" I asked her as I joined her in the kitchen and watched her pour coffee.

"Still trying to nail down where Joshua is, overseeing some issues down in Georgia, another three people are missing, and no one has any information on Portage. Same shit, different day." She turned and sipped from her cup.

"What are you hiding?" I had learned a long time ago to shoot straight with her. I got much further when I did.

"Nothing." She went to step around me, and I hopped in front of her and raised a brow. "I said nothing."

"Then why is your mind like a fortress? Not even Cameron can get into your head."

She looked surprised. "Really, huh? Wonder why." She moved around me. I followed her out of her kitchen and to her stairs that led to her roof patio. If she was going up there, maybe she wanted to tell me something. I followed, hoping that was the case. Upstairs she took a seat and stared out at the city.

"Seriously, Kristin, where is your mind?"

She laughed. "This is not the first time that I have blocked you, Angelina."

"Yeah, but this is the first time you have done so and been so melancholy. What is eating at you? Are you worried that we won't find Josh?"

"No, I know we will find him." She grew quiet and then released a massive stream of air. "I'm thinking about the past. Wondering what the purpose of those lessons were and wishing that I had Alex here to bounce things off of."

"So you're second-guessing yourself, huh?"

"Kind of, but more like wondering what Alex would do now. What would Alex do with this situation? What would Julian do?"

"I don't know. You would know better than me, but I do know that they trusted your opinion on almost everything. Both of them stood behind you all the time. That's why Alex said you would make a good leader when he was gone."

"What if one of them came back, Angelina? I mean, I know that Alex was dusted, and there is no chance, but what if Julian came back? He was supposed to be the next Master, but he walked away from it and gave it to Alex."

"I thought Julian was dusted, too. So why are you even thinking of this? It's not possible."

"Maybe it is possible," she said softly.

"What are you talking about, Kristin?"

She turned to me and seemed to be thinking over her words. "I found Julian's body after he died. He hadn't turned to ash as he fell. His body was broken and beaten, but his heart was intact. I put him into the morning sun."

"What? Why did you say he was gone forever then?"

"Because I had no clue what was going on at the time. I

almost staked him, but then I wondered if I didn't if he would come back to me."

"Well, it's been what, thirty-six years, and he hasn't."

"Thirty-five, and what if he didn't know he was a reborn, Angelina? What if he is like Hugh?"

"What if he is? Are you going to put your life on hold to search for him? He could be anywhere, or he could be dead for good."

She stared at her coffee mug. "What if he's not?"

I laughed. "Wow, you really are stuck on memory lane, aren't you? Look, if dear ole' dad were alive, I guarantee he would be searching for you, and he would have found you. It's not like you are a secret to anyone now. Everyone knows who you are."

"Yeah, maybe," she said softly and stared out into the night. "But what if I could find him?"

"What about Hugh?"

She didn't respond, just kept staring into the night.

I reached over and put my hand on her arm. "Kris, are you alright? Why is this bothering you so much?"

Kris turned to me, and I noticed her eyes change color, and then I blinked, and she was staring at me. I frowned as if I had missed something, but she suddenly smiled.

"So, I hear the plans for the dance club are going well. How much longer do you think it will take for it to be done?"

"I'd say two weeks. We have crews working twenty-four seven, so it's coming together quickly." I scanned the night; why do I feel like I missed something here?

"That's great; I'm looking forward to it." She stood. "Well, I have to get down to the office. I have a lot to get done." She stared down at me. "Thanks, Lena."

"For what?"

"For being here when I needed you to be."

"Okay," I said slowly, and she turned and walked away. Man, I needed to get this club done quickly so my sister could have some fun. Things were too serious right now. She needed to let down that hair of hers and unwind. Get a little crazy.

I let myself back into her apartment and went down the stairs. In her living room, I paused at the shelf again. Are you alive, Dad? I shook my head as I heard a sound behind me.

"Hey, Angelina. I thought you were Kristin."

"Good thing you didn't come out here in your birthday suit, then," I told him as I turned.

"You would have enjoyed that."

I hiked a brow. "You forget I have seen it before."

He chuckled. "Did your sister leave?"

"Yeah, she went down to her office." I wandered closer to him. "Everything okay with you two?"

"Sure, everything is fine," he replied but didn't look at me. Did I dare broach the subject with him?

No, obviously my sister was working through something and she needed some space. The only thing we could do was to give her that and be there when she was ready to talk or command.

"Okay, well, glad to hear that. I need to go. I have to go inspect what was done on the club today while we slept."

"I will see you down there in a little while."

"Sounds good," I called over my shoulder, and as I passed the shelf again, I glanced at it, and a shiver zipped down my spine. I frowned to myself as I let myself out the door and headed toward the elevator.

CHAPTER TWENTY-NINE

ZANDER

*S*aturday afternoon arrived, and I paced around my house. My bag was ready, and I stared at it, wondering if I was doing the right thing. Should I trust Gabe? I had always trusted him, or I should say Julian always trusted him, so why shouldn't I? I couldn't think of a reason.

Gabe was working with my father, so he wasn't trying to trap me. We had been close friends back when I lived another life, and he was willing to help me understand this. Since my talk with him, I had not seen Laura nor heard from my father. Both of them were suspiciously quiet. Was this whole thing part of his plan?

Did he think that I would be able to bring Kristin to him? Maybe that is exactly what he thought I would do. This had to be a trap, but if it were, wouldn't it be better to let me know?

I was still confused as to why Gabe had said that I should bond immediately. Was he talking about bonding to Kristin? Why the hell would I do that? Yeah, I know that once upon a time we were a thing, but we didn't know one another now.

Did he think that if I bonded with her, I could somehow

control her or get her to bend to my will? It was absurd to think, and I tried not to dwell on it.

I dialed the phone number that Gabe had left me, and the man who answered said very few words. "Your ride is on its way. Destroy your phone." The line went dead, and I was pretty sure that if I called the number again, no one would answer.

I stared at my phone as I walked into the kitchen. I set it on the counter and grabbed a hammer from under the sink. I stared down at the phone, remembering a time that I had smashed another one. A memory that had come back to me, and I knew it had something to do with running away, but I wasn't exactly sure why I had run away.

I took the hammer to the phone a few times and then set it down on the counter beside it, grabbed my bag, and stood at the door. The sun was still up, but getting close to setting. As soon as the transport arrived and opened the door, I rushed into it and got seated. The door closed, and I glanced back at my house one more time.

This might be a trap, and my father might be playing me, but for the first time in a long time, I felt that I had a purpose. I felt like once I spoke with her, I might understand things better. Unless this was a trap on her side and she had convinced Gabe to bring me to her for her own purposes.

There were so many unknowns here, but still, I sat back, knowing that soon, I might have some answers.

A phone rang a few minutes into the drive, and I glanced toward the driver. He put the security screen up between us, and I answered the phone that was in a cupholder.

"Yes?"

"You have a little ride, so sit back and relax. Anything you could need is available to you there."

"Where am I going again?"

"You're going to a house owned by the VMF, but don't worry, she's coming alone. No one knows that you will be there except your driver. He will drop you off and pick you up once you call him again."

"How long do I have?"

He hesitated. "I told her that she should expect to stay overnight. So at least twenty-four hours."

"Okay," I said softly. "You know, I'm putting a lot of trust into you, Gabe."

"I know." He sounded sad. "The things we do for the people we love."

"I guess," I replied. I hadn't ever been in love, at least in this life. Julian had been in love with two women, Kristin and Lyssa. However, the feelings he had for Kristin were oddly more than I could ever imagine feeling for someone. It made me wonder if Julian was right in the mind.

"Good luck, Zander."

"Thanks," I told him, and the line went dead. I set the phone down and looked out the window.

For hours, I stared out the window, and then as if I knew we were getting close to our destination, I started to get nervous. I shifted in the seat, wondering again if this was a trap, and fearing it was. Yet, I was also excited or anxious to see her face-to-face. To see if any more memories or feelings came back to me. If it were a trap, maybe it would be worth it once I understood more of what, or who, I was.

The transport pulled into a driveway and wove back into the woods and up a hill. The moment the house came into view, my heart began to race as pictures started to flood my mind.

The door of the transport opened, and I retrieved the phone and my bag and climbed out. I was barely out when the transport door began to close, and it zipped back down the hill.

The house in front of me was three stories, even though only two had windows. *The top floor is for the bedrooms*, I thought to myself. I glanced around, my eyes settling on the garage, and I instantly recalled two transports—no cars—back then, they were cars. One was dark blue, the other purple. One was hers, one mine.

I turned back to the front door; another memory slammed into me of an animal rushing toward me, a dog with long fur and caramel-colored eyes, happy to see me. Garda—his name was Garda, and he was her dog.

I went to the door, expecting it to be locked, but it wasn't. The knob turned easily in my hand, and I pushed it open and reached inside to where I knew the light switch would be. A bright light exploded out into the darkness, and I blinked as I looked up at the massive chandelier hanging in the entryway. I stepped in and closed the door; the entry was lined with stone as I knew it would be. I had stood right here and told Kristin that I hated her, wished she were dead. I didn't understand why I had done that, but I could remember that scene and the conflicting thoughts that ran through my mind.

I dropped my bag by the door and stepped farther into the house. The living room was on the left, the furniture different, but similar. On the bar was a bottle of Firefly Vodka. I smiled slightly; Kristin had always enjoyed drinking that.

I glanced down the hall and followed it back to the kitchen. After I turned the light on, I stood there as memories exploded around me. A woman on the counter, Alex cutting into her chest. Kristin at the fridge, drinking blood straight from the bag. Another man at the sink, his arms crossed as he glared at me. Trent. His name was Trent. I frowned; I didn't like Trent. I wasn't quite sure why, but I didn't.

More memories tore around inside of me, and I left the kitchen and headed to the stairs. I took them to the second floor, pausing at the landing and staring down toward the rooms at the other end. Bedrooms for other guests, one of them was a gym for Kristin to work off stress. Her office was straight ahead.

I stepped into the room, but it was no longer an office. It

was now a bedroom, and the desk, chairs, and couch that had once been in here were gone. Too bad, the sofa had been comfortable. I turned from the room and went back to the stairs.

I slowly took them, and at the top, my gaze went to the third door down. That had been her room. Across the hall was where I had slept. It was also the room where I had mated with Calista. Jesus, this was real. There is no way I could remember all of these things if it hadn't been.

I went to her room and pushed open the door. It was still decorated the same and a bit dusty, but it had been cleaned not too long ago. I stepped in, seeing ghosts in every direction. Her laughing, crying, kissing me. I went to the dresser on the far side, lifting the picture that was there. In it were Kristin, Trent, the man that I wasn't sure I liked, and Alex, but there was also another man in the picture, and I knew without a doubt that it was me—or Julian.

The eyes that stared back at me were identical to mine, and I didn't need a mirror to tell me that. I set the picture down, studying the man that I used to be. What would she think of the man that I was now?

Did it matter what she thought? A sound from downstairs captured my attention, and I went on high alert. I flashed to the steps and reached out. There was one presence downstairs—a female. I knew without a shadow of a doubt that it was her, and I slowly started to take the stairs.

I felt her, and I knew she felt me. As I rounded the landing and started down the flight to the ground floor, I saw her standing in the center of the entryway. Her long red hair cascaded around her shoulders, her eyes bright blue, her full lips parted. Her scent rose to me, and I almost stumbled down the stairs as I sucked it in like I was drowning. I paused, gathering my control as we stared at one another.

"Hello, Kristin."

She blinked, her mouth closing before she licked her lips and spoke softly. "Hello."

The sound of her voice washed over me, music to my ears, and I was able to move again. I took the stairs slowly, making sure not to startle her. She was on edge, wary. I reached out to her, but her mind was closed off. I could feel her power crackling under the surface—she was way more powerful than I had anticipated. If she wanted to destroy me, she could probably do it in the blink of an eye.

I paused a few feet away. "Thank you for coming."

She nodded and glanced around for a moment. "I'm afraid that I'm at a loss here. You seem to know who I am, but I don't know who you are."

I gave her a crooked smile and shuffled forward a few inches. "You know who I am, Kristin, and for the first time in thirty-five years, I finally know exactly who I am."

"Who?" She spoke, her voice not showing any emotion, but I saw it in her eyes. I felt it in the air; she was afraid. The mistress was unsure.

I didn't want her to fear me.

"You know who, Kris. I'm the man that you loved, the man that you mated with so many years ago, and then died for. The same one that you loved again when you came back. The man who said he would always love you."

"How do I know it's true? How do I know that you aren't someone else pretending to be him?"

I chuckled and stepped forward. We were only a foot apart now, and her strength continued to crackle around her. It bounced off of me, sometimes curling around my body, almost pulling me toward her.

"I know you, Kristin. I know you love peaches cut up in your pancakes, and that you hated not having a job when we were first mated. I know we mated by accident, but that I fell in love with you the moment I saw you at the bar that night. I never stopped loving you, even when you mated with Alex. Even after you mated with Trent, and even when I left you and went out west."

She blinked as if she were trying to hold back her emotions, and I continued. "I loved you even when I loved Lyssa, and you knew that; she knew that." I glanced away as a scene came back to me.

Her lying in a bed, filthy, barely alive, and me on that bed with her, feeding her, breaking the fragile bond that I had created with Lyssa. The scene changed, and I winced.

"You were there when I died. You saw Adam kill me." I frowned, thinking about how he worked for my father. Did my father know he was the one that had killed Julian? Did my father know that I was Julian?

Kristin shifted slightly from one foot to another, and I saw her fingers twitch. I reached out to touch her, my finger running down her cheek, and her eyes closed as she whimpered slightly.

I cupped her cheek. "I remember everything about you, Kristin. I remember this—this intense feeling that we had every single time that we touched. It was undeniable."

Tears filled her eyes as she leaned into my palm, and the two of us were drawn together so very slowly. Our breath began to mingle when she tensed and pulled back suddenly. The energy around her turned almost visible as her eyes scanned the room.

Her voice was different, more intense, no longer soft and emotional. "Did you come alone?"

I nodded, and then I too felt it. Other presences were closing in on us. "Did you set me up?" I said to her.

"I did not. I am pretty sure this trap was set for both of us." She grabbed my face, her eyes turning a liquid silver. "Do you trust me?"

"Do I have a choice?"

She shook her head, and before I knew what she was going

to do, she twirled me around and put me up against the wall. She put her lips to mine and nipped at my bottom lip with her fangs. She sucked from my lip and moaned. *Bond immediately,* the words filled my mind suddenly, and I knicked her tongue. Her blood mixed with mine with such an intensity that I thought I would drop to the floor. I wrapped my arms around her, and our initial sharing of blood turned into a passionate kiss.

"Trust me, Julian," she whispered into my mind just a moment before the door behind her blew off the hinges, and then an electrical blast took us to the ground.

CHAPTER THIRTY

HUGH

I was learning new things every day and making friends along the way. Well, at least with everyone but Rex. That man kept his distance from me, and after trying a few times to bridge it, I gave up. He could think what he wanted, I didn't care.

What I did care about was helping Kristin and the rest of them find this facility. I felt personally responsible for it since I had been in charge of the task force that had gathered the information. Kristin said she didn't blame me, but she had distanced herself over the last couple of days, so I had to wonder if she was being honest.

My boss was still staying at the hotel, and word had gotten out about him disappearing. I received a phone call two days after we brought him here from Tom Singer, who wanted to know if I had spoken with him. I told him that I knew nothing.

Eventually, it was going to come out that I was not coming back to work, and not only that, but that I had switched teams. They were going to have to rethink a few things because I knew how they worked. Hell, I set into play how they worked. We would have the advantage for a little while, but not much longer.

Clayton had asked us when we wanted to announce our mating to the public officially, but I told him we needed to hold back a little while longer, at least until the news got back to my job. Once we made it public, a lot of things were going to change.

Angelina thought it would be a good idea to wait until the club opened, then we could throw a great big Grand Opening of Compulsion. That was the name she had decided on when Kristin said she didn't care.

So it was decided that in a couple of weeks, my time off would be ending, and I would let them in on my little secret, along with announcing to the world that I was now the mate of the illustrious mistress.

I thought Kristin would be more excited, but she remained reserved. She kept herself behind closed doors, working until late in the morning and then up again in the middle of the afternoon. Was it Josh missing that was upsetting her so much? Or the inability to find him and the others?

We had barely had any alone time together until Saturday afternoon. I woke to find her lying on her side, watching me. I smiled sleepily at her. "Why are you watching me?"

"Because I can," she said saucily.

A moment later, I had moved to cover her as I pushed her to her back. "Yeah, well, then I can do this." I kissed her slowly as my hand brushed down her side, and she arched toward me.

"Make love to me, Hugh." Her words were husky, filled with an emotion that I didn't quite understand, but I wasn't going to look a gift horse in the mouth. For days I had wanted her, but I had waited.

I made love to Kristin in a way we had never done before. It was slow and gentle and filled with feelings that I didn't want to question. When we were done, I curled up behind her and held her tightly for a few moments, savoring my time with her. She sighed and shifted out of my grasp, turning to me, and I saw her eyes flash silver. A moment later, she was strolling across the bedroom and into the bathroom.

I didn't see her again until almost midnight, and she was in her office, staring at the picture from forty years ago. She tried to smile at me, but it was obviously forced. "Hey, you have time to come down to eat?"

"Um, no. Sorry. I am about to go into a meeting."

"Alright, I'll see you later then." I turned to leave.

"Hugh!" I stopped and twisted back to her as she stood. She came to stand in front of me, searching my eyes. "Thank you."

"For what?"

"For being a great guy, for being willing to take so many chances and trust me blindly."

"Of course." I cupped her cheek. "Are you alright, Kris? You seem oddly reserved."

She put her hand over my heart. "I'm fine, or I will be soon. I just need to work through something." As she spoke, her gaze skittered back to the picture, and then she leaned forward and kissed me tenderly.

She stood there as I left, and I could feel her watching me as I walked down the hallway. When I got to the corner, I looked back at her, and she smiled and waved.

She was acting so oddly. I was going to have to see if Angelina could try to speak with her again. Something was up. I didn't know her well, but I knew something was not right.

We got busy with some new information, and I asked if anyone had told Kristin about it, but Lorna quickly stepped in and said that the mistress was still in a meeting.

It wasn't until almost three-thirty that something hit me right in the gut and made me grab on to the wall as I walked down the hallway toward Kristin's office. At first, it felt like a rush of passion, so overwhelming that it almost turned me on, but it quickly turned to a thirst that broke my fangs from my gums. Something was happening, but I didn't understand it. A moment later, a sliver of fear raced through me and then pain. So much pain that I almost went to my knees as I sucked in a breath.

"Hugh!" Clayton had come out of his office. "What the hell is going on?"

I stared at him, trying to interpret what I had felt. "Where is Kristin?"

He shook his head. "I don't know."

"Where the hell is Kristin? We have to find her, Clay. She's in trouble!"

"What?" Clayton helped me get to my feet, just as the stairwell door burst open, and Angelina rushed in, stopping in front of me.

"Did you feel it?"

I nodded. "Yes, I did. What the hell was that?"

"Kristin is in trouble."

"Where is she?" Clayton asked as more people began to join us, and Clayton started spouting out commands, one to find Lainey. A moment later, Lainey came rushing down the hallway looking alarmed.

"Who was she meeting with?"

She shook her head. "I don't know. She told me she had to run an errand."

"Run an errand?" Angelina echoed in a high-pitched voice. "When has she ever run a fucking errand!"

"Lainey, think." Clayton took her by the shoulders. "Did she tell you anything else?"

"No, I swear, she didn't."

"She wouldn't have gone after Josh alone, would she?" Jett asked as he stood on the outskirts of our group.

I pushed past everyone and went into her office, going to her desk and starting to move things around. There wasn't much, and I growled. "Where the fuck is she? She's in trouble. I felt—" I paused, not sure how much to say.

"Did you feel passion, Hugh? Before the fear and pain, did you feel the passion?" Angelina asked.

"Yes, that's exactly what I felt, but there was something else."

Angelina turned and moved to the picture on the wall near the door. "He really is alive."

"What are you talking about?"

"We don't know that for sure." A voice spoke from the door, and we all turned to see Lorna standing there.

Angelina glared at her. "What the hell do you know about this?"

"Kristin got a message that he had been reborn and that he wanted to see her."

"Who are you talking about?" I asked at the same time that Angelina slammed Lorna back against the wall.

"Where the hell is my sister?"

"I don't know, Angelina. She told me not to say anything unless she didn't make it back."

"Where did she go?" I asked. "Who the hell was she with?" I shouted.

Lorna turned her head toward me as Angelina began to lessen the pressure. "Julian, she's with Julian, or whoever he is now."

"Julian?" I repeated. "I thought he was dead."

Angelina blinked and then blinked again, and then she shook her head. "Oh, that bitch!"

"What?" Clayton asked as Angelina started pacing and put her hand up. Finally, she stopped and slammed her hands on her hips.

"My sister compelled me today to forget this conversation until I needed to remember."

"What conversation?" Clayton asked before I could.

"She told me that Julian might be alive and that she was going to meet with him."

"How the hell would she know that he was alive—or could be? I thought his body was ashed when he died," Clayton growled.

Angelina shook her head. "No, she told me this morning that she had found his body and that she had laid him to rest in the sun. She said she watched him go up in flames and recovered his things before coming home where she found out that Lyssa was also dead."

Lorna nodded. "She told me that, too. She said she didn't want to bring his body back if my mom were still alive because she didn't want her to see him the way he was."

I winced. "So he could be a reborn?"

They all looked at me, and Angelina nodded. "Yes, he would be."

"Does anyone know where she went?" Jett asked as Rex came to join us.

"What's going on?"

"Your mother is missing," Lena stated.

"Missing? Wait! How? Did they come into the building and get her?"

"No, your mother went on a field trip, and we don't know where she is," Angelina stated sassily.

"We do know that she's in trouble now, though," I stated.

"How do you know that?"

"Because the last thing I felt from her was pain, and then she disappeared."

Angelina nodded. "But there was something else, right before that."

"What?" Clayton asked.

Angelina glanced around the room, winced slightly, and then directed her words to Clayton. "She bonded to someone seconds before."

"Is that what I felt?"

Angelina peered my way and nodded, looking almost sorry. "I could feel the bond take hold, and I know that feeling."

"What feeling?"

"I know what Kristin and Julian feel like when they are bonded."

I sank into Kristin's chair. "So, she's missing. She's with her past mate and lover, bonded to him now, and now something has happened to her. Does anyone know who the hell Julian might have been reborn as?"

Blank stares were returned to me. "Great, just fucking great," I muttered as I wiped a hand over my face.

Cora rushed into the room. "Who felt her?"

Angelina spoke up. "Both Hugh and I, why?"

"Show me, and I can tell you if it's the same as when Josh disappeared."

Angelina stuck her arm out, and Cora bit down as Lena closed her eyes. A moment later, she closed the puncture wounds. "That is the same pain that I got from Josh. It was almost like an electrical burst."

"Like a Taser?" I asked and thought about it. Oddly enough, that was what it felt like, only fifty times worse. "You're right; it was like a Taser."

"So the humans have her," Rex growled. "They are so fucking done now."

Clayton clapped a hand on Rex's shoulder. "Now hold on a minute before you go off on warp speed. If they have her, then we have a good idea where. We just need a little bit more information, and we can go after her. Your mother is smart; she knows what's she doing. If she bonded to Julian, or whoever he is, then you can bet she did it for a purpose."

They started talking amongst themselves, and I tuned out, staring at the picture as I thought back on our time earlier today. She had known this was going to happen. When we made love, was she saying goodbye, or telling me she'd be back?

Suddenly, a scene played out in my mind from earlier this morning when we were in bed.

"I know you aren't going to understand this, and you're going to think that I have gone behind your back, but I'm not doing it on purpose. I need to see this through, and I will explain it to you when I return. Something big is gonna happen, Hugh, and I need you to remain focused and stick to my sister." Kristin paused and swallowed tightly. "I know that Portage compelled you to come to me. That you are only mated to me because of that, not because you wish to be. Go to Angelina and have her break your compulsion. If it is your wish, come together with her in blood and body. Promise me that if something happens to me, you'll go to her and convince her this is the best thing. Bond with her, Hugh, or mate with her if that is what your heart wishes. I will not hold you if you wish to be with her."

Kristin had touched my face. "Thank you for what you have given me. For the power that you have filled me with beyond what others are aware of. You will not remember this until either I return, or you find out the truth of where I have gone. I am not doing this to hurt you; I care very much for you. I am doing this because Julian is part of my destiny, Hugh. Bond with Angelina and find me." She snapped her fingers, and I remember her getting out of bed and walking away from me.

"Well, son of a bitch!" I muttered, and all eyes turned to me. "She fucking compelled me too."

CHAPTER THIRTY-ONE

KRISTIN

*W*hen I got back to the hotel, I was going to have hell to pay. I hadn't compelled Lorna, but I did my sister, Hugh, Jett, Paxton, Conner, and Lainey. I was pretty sure that my sister and Hugh would take it the hardest.

I had enlisted Lorna's help to get me a transport and assist me to get out of the building undetected. After I told her why I needed it, she was happy to help. Julian had been like a father to her. She had been heartbroken to lose both her mother and Julian in one night.

As the transport took me out of the city and toward Fawn Hollow, I hoped that I was making the right decision. My mind ran back over Gabe's phone call, and his comment about doing anything he could for a person he loved. There was no doubt in my mind. Olivia was in dire trouble, and Gabe needed my help.

In order for me to help, he needed me to be here. Why? Was Julian really going to be there, or was that whole story made up to entice me to come? I prayed it was not. I had waited too long for his return.

By the time we hit the driveway to the VMF, I was a nervous wreck, but I forced myself to remain calm. I climbed out, staring up at the house and the few lights that were on. There were so many memories before me, so much pain, love, loss in this house.

I could feel someone inside, could feel a presence that called to me, and I followed it. I slowly entered, making sure that there was only one person here. He was on the third floor when I came in, and I heard him crossing the floor to the stairs and then taking them down slowly. Too fucking slowly. Was he as nervous as I was? Was it really Julian? It felt like his signature, and his leather and cinnamon scent was drifting through the entryway. I glanced down at the backpack on the floor near the door. The scent was strong coming off of it, but that could be my imagination.

When Julian stepped into view, my eyes ate him up. I wanted to run to him, to hold him, to breathe him in. He was different, and yet the same, although as much as I wanted to believe it was him, I feared this was all part of a trap.

Only the memories that he shared, the words that he spoke, the way he laughed, the look in his eye all told me that this was real. My Julian had returned to me, and I was ready to throw myself into his arms, but I still held back.

"You were there when I died. You saw Adam kill me."

When he touched my cheek, I felt it travel down my spine, deep into my soul. I remembered this touch; I craved this touch. He cupped my cheek. "I remember everything about you, Kristin. I remember this."

I couldn't help myself as my eyes began to fill with moisture, and I leaned into his touch. I had waited too long for this, and now he was back.

We leaned forward, and I could imagine the feel of his lips on mine. It didn't matter that he looked different, inside he was the same man I had loved for around eighty years.

I closed the distance, prepared to remind him of how we felt about one another when I felt a tickle on the edge of my mind. I paused and focused on it.

"Bond! Now! Kristin, hurry!" I jerked back, feeling many people converging on us. As I looked around, I tried to locate a way out, but the house was surrounded. It had been a trap, but I felt no animosity coming from Gabe. He was tense, nervous, afraid that we would be hurt, but he also had fear for Olivia.

"Did you come alone?" I asked him quickly.

He nodded, and then I knew he felt it too. His eyes darkened. "Did you set me up?"

"I did not. I am pretty sure this trap was set for both of us." I took hold of his face. "Do you trust me?" Please say yes, I begged silently! We don't have time for me to explain!

"Do I have a choice?"

I shook my head and put him against the wall so that my back was to the door. I kissed him, but I also took his blood, and it took only a moment for him to do the same. I was about to urge him to do it when he took the initiative.

Our blood mixed in our mouths, and we both swallowed, pulling it deep into our bodies. I took our last moment together to change the kiss to one I had dreamed of and whispered into his mind, *"Trust me, Julian."*

I didn't even know his proper name. I had no clue where he had been, how he had been raised, but that didn't matter. As the door blasted open and hammered us into the stone wall, I knew that no matter what was going to happen, Julian and I would survive it.

I could already feel our blood binding together, building inside of me as we slumped to the ground. I cracked open my eyes to see him lying there within arm's reach. I reached for him, but a booted foot stopped my progress as it stepped between us. My gaze drifted up the cowboy boot to the man's face as I rolled to my back. In his gaze was fear, sorrow, and love.

My mind started to shut down, but not before my last thought raced through my mind. No matter what happened, Julian and I would make it through. Our time had finally come, and God help the people who tried to come between us.

THE END

Now in the hands of the enemy forces, Kristin and Zander might be together, but being captured by sadistic terrorists will not allow their reunion to go as planned.

With Angelina, Hugh, Cameron, Clayton, Rex, and the rest of the gang trying to locate them, they must work fast to free them before Portage makes his move to take over the breed. Make sure to join us for *Zander: Blue Blood Reborn* for the continuation of the saga.

BLUE BLOOD RETURNS SERIES

The Blue Blood Returns Series is an adult paranormal romance with sexual situations, violence, language, and does contain a cliffhangers that lead right into the next book. While this is a new series, it does spin off of the *My Blood Runs Blue Series*.

The My Blood Runs Blue Series

My Blood Runs Blue, Book 1

Officer Kristin Greene has always felt that something was missing from her life. Although her job with the Fawn Hollow Township Police Department keeps her busy, she still feels like there is something else out there for her.

She soon finds herself investigating a homicide where a young woman has had her throat ripped out. As she begins to dig for the answers, she finds herself thrown into a world she didn't know ever existed.

When the two strong and silent men walk into her life, she finds herself being pulled into a love triangle that has been going on longer than she has been alive. Who are they and why do they keep calling her Calista?

Join Kristin as she fights to learn the truth about the recent murder, the two seductive men who have entered into her life and the real truth about herself.

The Pulse of Blue Blood, Book 2
The Pulse of Blue Blood is a short story that should be read AFTER My Blood Runs Blue. This story of 17K words is the back story to Kristin & Calista. Reading this story before reading My Blood Runs Blue will spoil many plot points.

In My Blood Runs Blue, you were introduced to Kristin, Julian, and Alexander, and you also learned a little about Calista.

Now take a trip back in time to learn more about the decisions that Calista made in her choice between Julian and Alexander.

Learn about her relationship with Julian, and why you choose Alexander at the end of My Blood Runs Blue. You'll also learn the way she caused her untimely death.
The Pulse of Blue Blood is a short story to be read after reading My Blood Runs Blue.

Blue Blood for Life, Book 3
After a month off, Kristin comes back to work happier then she's been in a long time. Her new status in life has her solving crimes faster and better than she ever could before.

When Alex goes missing, Kristin finds she finally has to reveal the secrets of her life to her friends. Will they be able to stand beside her after they learn all that she has hidden from them?

Julian and Gabe stand beside her faithfully as they try to locate Alex. They are surprised to find Trent already in Fawn Hollow, but know that Trent may be the only one to do what Alex has asked them to do. As one more choice is taken away from Kristin, she attempts to make the best of it, but finds herself drawn to Trent in a way Julian and Alexander could never compare to.

Trent goes to work with Kristin to keep her safe but will he be able to handle all that her police world entails? Can he handle the side of her that she reveals, the one that Alex and Julian know nothing about? When Kristin and Trent uncover the connection between her job and the kidnapping, they are finally able to put the pieces together, but can they get to Alex fast enough? Will Kristin be able to handle rescuing Alex and all that she learns in the process?

Join Kristin, Julian, Trent and Alexander as they dive into a new mystery that will have you turning the pages quickly to find out who is responsible and how Kristin's life is forever changed once again.

Mixing the Blue Blood, Book 4
Officer Kristin Greene returns along with the rest of the characters you have grown to love. Only this time, it's not just her life on the line. Now the entire breed's existence is in danger.

Olivia Newman has been Kristin's best friend for years and loves the new life that Kristin is living. Her relationship with

Gabriel is bittersweet, and she knows that because she is human, a future between them can never really last.

Gabriel Montgomery takes his position in the Vampire Military Force seriously and never expected to have such intense feelings for a human woman. When Olivia is kidnapped, Gabe, Kristin, and the gang realize they have stumbled upon a human trafficking ring. Only this ring isn't for sex. The leaders of this ring are hell-bent on destroying the breed.

Can they rescue Olivia and save their future before old enemies return and destroy the breed? Find out in Mixing the Blue Blood.

Blue Bloods Final Destiny, Book 5
Julian Hutchinson walked away from it all: his job, his friends and her. As Julian drives out west, he randomly stops at a roadside tavern and runs into some people from his past.

Ellie Lakin helps her father around the tavern as she raises her fifteen-year-old daughter, Lorna. When Julian walks into the bar, Ellie's past crush on him hits full force, but even she can tell that he is far from ready to be involved with anyone.

As Julian and Ellie grow their friendship their past romance is rekindled. When Julian's past comes back to haunt him, and an old enemy shows up in town, Julian knows a showdown is imminent. Will Julian be able to deal with his past, and his enemy without destroying the new life he has created.

The gang is back for one final book where lines are drawn and quickly crossed, and Julian and Kristin will have to work together one last time to save people that they care about.

The Blue Blood Returns Series:

Kristin: Blue Blood Returns Book 1

It's been forty years since the gang was together in Blue Bloods Final Destiny, and many things have changed. Lives have been lost, mates are different, and the breed is on the verge of war. This war isn't just between the two factions within the vampire race, but now includes the humans who have learned of their existence.

With the Mistress, Kristin, at the helm, the tension is growing, and the elders are pushing for a change. The U.S. government wants information on the breed, and Joseph Portage, Kristin's newest enemy, is lurking in the shadows.

Hugh McMurphy heads a task force that is determined to get the vampire race under control and learn what they can do. When Kristin and Hugh find themselves pulled toward one another, the only option is to make Hugh her human consort.

It's not until she tastes his blood that she realizes Hugh is more than originally thought, and with Portage's men wreaking havoc on the town, she realizes that something drastic needs to happen.

Can Kristin and the new gang figure things out before a major transition occurs, or will Kristin and her sister get blindsided by the taste of blood?

Hugh: Blue Blood Compelled Book 2
Take a short trip back in time to find out how Hugh got involved with his special task force and then learned about the hidden society before he was summoned to meet with Joseph Portage and began a new mission.

Kristin knows that there is more going on than meets the eye with Hugh. Now she not only has to deal with the issues of the breed, but also the secrets of her new and powerful mate. A warning from an old friend not taken seriously will put Kristin in a tailspin as the past and present converge in the flash of the strobes and the thump of the base.

With the rest of the VMF gang working to find Portage and protecting Kristin, there are ups and downs for all of them, but Josh is hell-bent on figuring out what Hugh's secret is.

Portage has his way in now, but that is only step one of his plan to control Kristin and take over the breed. While Zander continues to get frustrated with the dreams and his father, he finally decides to take off on his own and figure things out. It's not until he arrives in Philadelphia that he will start to find answers—but they will change everything.

Zander: Blue Blood Reborn, Book 3

Zander and Kristin come face to face, both being led back to the VMF house in Fawn Hallow by a friend, but is he an enemy in disguise?
    Now in the hands of the enemy forces, Kristin and Zander

might be together, but being captured by sadistic terrorists will not allow their reunion to go as planned.

With Angelina, Hugh, Cameron, Clayton, Rex, and the rest of the gang trying to locate them, they must work fast to free them before Portage makes his move to take over the breed. Make sure to join us for Zander: Blue Blood Reborn for the continuation of the saga.

Releases March 2021.

Lena: Blue Blood Desired, Book 4 (late 2021)

ABOUT THE AUTHOR

Stacy Eaton is a USA Today Best Selling author and began her writing career in October of 2010. Stacy took an early retirement from law enforcement after over fifteen years of service in 2016, with her last three years in investigations and crime scene investigation to write full time.

Stacy resides in southeastern Pennsylvania with her husband, who works in law enforcement, and her teen daughter. She also has a son who is currently serving in the United States Navy and has two grandchildren.

Be sure to visit www.stacyeaton.com for updates and more information on her books.

Sign up for all the latest information on Stacy's Newsletter!

ALSO BY STACY EATON

Paranormal Romance:

My Blood Runs Blue Series

My Blood Runs Blue, Book 1 **

The Pulse of Blue Blood, Book 2 (Short Story) **

Blue Blood for Life, Book 3 **

Mixing the Blue Blood, Book 4 **

Blue Bloods Final Destiny, Book 5 **

The Return of Blue Blood Series:

Kristin: Blue Blood Returns, Book 1 ***

Hugh: Blue Blood Compelled, Book 2 ***

Zander: Blue Blood Reborn, Book 3 (2021) ***

Lena: Blue Blood Desired, Book 4 (2021)

Garda ~ Welcome to the Realm

Domestic Violence – Crime - Suspense:

Whether I'll Live or Die**

Barbara's Plea

You're Not Alone**

Romantic Suspense:

Liveon ~ No Evil **

Second Shield **

Distorted Loyalty**

Six Days of Memories **

Second Shield II: The Return ***

Contemporary Romance:

Tempt Me Too**

Finding the Strength

Finding Love in Special Places:

Stacy's Short Story Series

Finding Love on Christmas Vacation

Finding Love on the Summer Surf

Finding Love with Dear Santa

Finding Love with a Champagne Toast

Heart of the Family Series

Mistletoe & Cocoa Kisses, Book 1 **

Roses & Champagne Kisses, Book 2 **

Orchids & Hurricane Kisses, Book 3 **

Carnations & Hot Toddy Kisses, Book 4 **

Heal Me Series

Cured, Book 1 **

Revived, Book 2

Mended, Book 3

Rescued, Book 4

The Celebration Series

Tangled in Tinsel, Book 1 **

Tears to Cheers, Book 2 **

Heathens to Hearts, Book 3 **

Rainbows Bring Riches, Book 4 ***

Sweet as Sugar, Book 5 ***

Making Mom Mad, Book 6 ***

Sparklers or Spankings, Book 7 ***

Raffles to Rattles, Book 8 ***

Flirting with Fireworks, Book 9 ***

Working under Wheels, Book 10 ***

Masquerading at Midnight, Book 11 ***

Blessings & Beans, Book 12 ***

Velvet & Vows, Book 13 ***

The Celebration Series Box Sets:

Part One: Books 1-5

Part Two: Books 6-9

Part Three: Books 10-13

The Sometimes Series:

Sometimes You Win, Book 1**

Sometimes You Lose, Book 2**

Sometimes You Play The Game, Book 3**

The Sometimes Series: Win, Lose & Play Set **

Pleasure Your Fantasies Series

Mistletoe Fantasies, Book 1 **

Whispered Fantasies, Book 2

Secret Fantasies, Book 3

The Twisted Love Series

with Amy Manemann Co-Author

Love Lorn, Book 1 (Manemann)**

Love Torn, Book 2 (Eaton)**

Love Inked, Book 3

Love Drowned, Book 4

Love Carved, Book 5

Love Trapped, Book 6 (Coming Soon)

Love Crossed, Book 7 (Coming Soon)

Love Twisted, Book 8 (Coming Soon)

Love Lies, Book 9 (Coming Soon)

Rise Again Warrior Series

Mission: Believe, Book 1 **

Mission: Accept, Book 2 **

Mission: Repair, Book 3

Loving a Young Series

Wesley, Book 1

Henley, Book 2

Huntley, Book 3

Riley, Book 4

The Unexpected Series

Unexpected Packages

Unexpected Arrivals

Unexpected Trouble

Unexpected Storms

Unexpected Desires

Unexpected Ties (coming soon)

** These books are also available on Audio

*** These books are coming to Audio soon

List Updated 2-3-21